The Madrinha

Madelyn Gregory

Published by Madelyn Gregory, 2024.

THE MADRINHA

First edition. October 16, 2024.

Written by Madelyn Gregory.

I

Jose'Antonio Silva Pires was a New Bedford fisherman who never came home from sea. Maria Esperanca de Macedo Pires was his 54 year old widow . Men were lost at sea almost every year and over thirty three years ago on August 13th it was his fate and that of his best friend Nuno Franciso Castro. Maria and Matilda, Nuno's wife, became widows in an undeclared sisterhood that is born in grief and determination. They wore their widowhood like a badge. Their uniform was the black clothes they would wear for the rest of their lives as did all Portuguese widows. Maria lived in the same neighborhood where her parents had brought her and her brother 40 years ago from the Azores. She never had children, but she had so many godchildren that now everyone called her "Madrinha" (godmother). She was a 5 foot tall dynamo. She was wide, strong and wise. Her dark curly hair had no hint of grey, thanks to Steph the new girl at the salon on Dartmouth Street a few blocks away.

It was May 13th and as many Portuguese Catholics knew, the 13th of the months from May until October are holy. Their belief is that the Virgin Mary appeared to the three young shepherd children in a grotto in Fatima, Portugal on the 13th of those months and a special miracle on the last apparition which was in October. These days are celebrated with elaborate parades and processions and all day festivals or *festas* as they are called with houses and streets decorated. The city of New Bedford Massachusetts is no exception.

Like every day except Sundays, Maria's phone rang by 10 a.m. Whenever she tried to answer the phone, she hung up on the caller instead. She could not get used to these cell phones. Caller ID read that this call was from Connie. She called back, but all she could hear was sobbing. What Maria gathered was that Connie was having trouble getting her husband Manny dressed and into his wheelchair to get to the procession in time. Manny knew that this year would provide many miracles and he just wanted to hold his rosary beads up to the statue of the Virgin Mary as it passed their street and maybe he would be healed from the stroke he had 4 years ago. Maria knew that his wife Connie would also appreciate a miracle so she did not have to bathe and dress this man every day.

Maria lived only a block from the daSilva's, so she walked there. The crowd had already gathered to watch the procession. The streets had been blocked off by the police since 6 a.m. No cars on the streets so they could be decorated with flower petals in the designs that had been marked in chalk since last night. Maria walked quickly. She got to the daSilva's house just in time to hear Connie swearing in Portuguese at Manny as she passed the window.. She walked into the side door of the well cared for tenement house as Connie hurled the folded walker toward the door and it landed at Maria's feet; without missing a beat, she stepped over the walker and into the room.

"We have not time to waste, Conceicao," she barked in Portuguese at Connie as she deftly pulled the ironed shirt onto Manny, she put his arms over her shoulders and pulled his pants up over the diaper that he was already wearing. Together the two of them shuttled Manny out the door to the wheelchair that waited in the driveway. "*Vamos la,* let's go," Maria called out over her shoulder. Connie tried to catch up as she ran as quickly as she could in her *chinelos* [1].

They could hear the bands playing which meant they had stepped off from the church already. The sidewalk was filled with people. Men who worked all week in construction or on the fishing boats were now in suits and ties and women were in their Sunday best; colorful as always except for the widows who wore black. Even though the crowd had parted for the wheelchair, the procession was moving too quickly for them to get to the next corner before the statue came by. The first communion children were already passing the corner, girls in white dresses and boys in white or blue suits, hands in prayer position, marching at a slow, but steady pace.

Maria decided to bring the wheelchair right into the street with a breathless Connie behind them. She got to the street corner just as the men carrying the statue did. The procession was stopped and as they started again, Maria pushed the wheelchair alongside those who shouldered the statue of the Virgin Mary, but Manny could not raise his arm with his rosary. There was a boy about 10 years old standing at the curb. Maria grabbed the sleeve of his t-shirt without a word. "Here push the chair," she said. The boy looked confused, but as Maria asked as she ran alongside, she wrapped the string of rosary beads around Manny's hand and almost dislocated his shoulder to pull his hand as close to the statue as she could. He almost cold-cocked the man struggling to hold up his corner of the stand.

They could stop now and Maria released the boy from the chore she had drafted him to do. His grandmother came running up as they returned to the sidewalk. Maria patted the boy's head and he shrugged his shoulder away from her, but she slipped him a $5 bill and said "Good boy, God will bless you." The boy's grandmother knew Maria and was grateful that her grandson had been chosen to help with such a kind act. Connie, gasping for air was now convinced , if she weren't before, that Maria was an angel among them. "Maria, I have goat meat for you in the freezer at home. Please let me give you some and wine. I still have a few gallons from last year's wine in the basement." "No need," said Maria. "I have 15 gallons left. I will be giving two gallons to Father Avila for auctions or raffles and I will have plenty until fall. There is moonshine. We are making a new still in the greenhouse soon. I will take the goat meat. We must get Manny home and feed him before we go to the church. We need to help with raffles and selling *malasadas* (Portuguese fried and sugared dough).

II

The feast at the church yard lasted for hours. When the children got tired of playing the games, eating linguica, hot dogs and ice cream and riding bikes back and forth to Ashley park, a block away, they went back home almost ready for bed. Parents had spent plenty of money on food and raffles and listened to the band play music. They danced *chamaritas* and sang along with the music and spent money like water on raffles just to donate the prizes back. There was plenty of money for the scholarships and church repairs. Maria always made sure the moneys were well spent. She was mother hen to all.

By 5 p.m., the crowd had dwindled and the families were packing up children. The men and women of the committee spread out like a small swarm of bees and cleared the grounds in less than an hour. The broom brigade followed the men taking down the booths. As the feast grounds were being organized, Maria tended to Father Avila. Just as he staggered back from the rectory Maria sidetracked him. She put her hand on his shoulder and told him how glad she was that the weather was so pleasant as she steered him back to the rectory. "Father Avila, you have worked so hard today. Be proud of the day. *Nossa Senhora's* (Our Lady's) celebration turned out well, but you must rest." He nodded obediently as he walked into the kitchen door to the rectory. Maria turned and called over her shoulder, "Father do not look for whiskey under the sink, it is not there." She smiled to herself as she left.

Maria returned to the home she had lived in since 6 years before her husband was lost and all the years since. She walked into the little cottage. Who would have thought among all these tenement houses there would be this tiny estate. Behind the house was the greenhouse where she grew herbs and started plants every spring and made moonshine every fall. There was a small chicken coop with four chickens and a rabbit coop with two large rabbits. The basement of the house of course had a kitchen where she cooked the fish and octopus often especially on Fridays and where the women came to drink coffee and wine and gossip while the men sat at the picnic tables under that grape arbor and drink and play cards. There was a large tv in the finished basement with a large closet under the stairs where the toys were hidden for the days when she cared for neighborhood children and there was the wine closet for the barrels of wine and the shelves filled with the produce that she and her friends canned. The yard was big enough to have a small fruitful garden. The hydrangeas and roses surrounded the house and so many other colors, too, foxglove, bright red cockscomb, and every summer the window boxes on the porch rail and large pots on the porch and on the stairs bloomed with many begonias and pansies.

III

Maria's weekdays were always busy. She babysat and helped at the church and helped wherever else she could, so when Julia called on Sunday afternoon and said she was coming over, Maria got out the platter of sweet rice, a pot of strong coffee, a bottle of wine, some cheese and the fresh baked bread that she had brought home just that morning after Mass. Julia was even shorter, wider and younger than Maria, but she looked older and she was obviously not happy. Maria met her at the door and embraced her as tightly as she could. They kissed on each cheek and Maria brought her into the kitchen. They did not speak and Julia started crying softly at first and then loud wailing and a river of tears. "Tell me," was all Maria said. Julia said tomorrow her youngest son, Jacinto, was going away to jail. His sentence was at least 6 years for buying drugs and ICE would probably be there to deport him. Jacinto was born in the Acores and she brought him here at 2 months old. Whatever would he do in a Portuguese prison? There they only give one meal a day and they do not even supply toilet paper or soap. He does not even speak Portuguese well enough to go shopping here in a local shop. And she cried, "And he is so pretty! He will be someone's 'girlfriend.'" Maria listened and refilled Julia's cup of coffee several times before she took it away and gave the glass of wine. "I talk to him. He is in jail?" No, Julia said, they had to surrender him in the morning. Julia knew that Maria would know the right things to say to him to keep him strong. She drank only one or two more glasses of wine before she got up to leave. Julia tied her kerchief over her silver curls and weaved her way to the door. "I will walk home with you," Maria offered, but before she could gather her purse and sweater, Julia was gone.

Maria got her purse and a small pad of paper and a nice pen and walked over to Julia's house. It was only about 2 streets away to Bonney Street which gave Maria more time to think of what to say to the Borges family and especially Jacinto. The sidewalk in front of the house was swept and neat as was the walkway to the side door of the tenement house as it always was. She walked through the gate in the anchor fence which was newly painted and knocked twice and walked in. There was a large dining table in what most homes would have as a living room and there sat Julia with her box of tissues and Jacinto looking less than his 19 years and as scared as he could be. Mr. Antonio Borges acknowledged Maria with a nod and a grunt when she walked in and he promptly got up from the table and left. He seemed to be 2 of his 3 sheets to the wind already. Julia apologized and said he was having a hard time with the situation and was ashamed of his son, being caught buying drugs.

Julia gave Jacinto a tray of cookies and told him to bring it downstairs and wait there for Maria. He took the tray and walked zombie-like to the top of the stairs and trudged down slowly. When she saw that they were alone, Julia turned to Maria, "I want another glass of wine." Maria took Julia's hands, " You can have some coffee while I am downstairs with Jacinto. Pray with me. Lord, God, Jesus, we beg you to keep this boy safe on his journey no matter where it leads him. Keep him far from the evilness of this world until he is safely in your arms." Maria looked Julia in the eye, bloodshot as it was and told her, "With Jesus' help he will be kept from harm. Trust."

Maria got up from the table and quickly disappeared down the stairs to the basement. The basement was not what most people would recognize as a basement. The walls were tiled in beautiful blue and white tiles and there was an entertainment area with comfortable couches around a large coffee table. There were linen doilies on the table and candy dishes and there was a full bar that was gleaming and polished. Maria went behind the bar and retrieved a jug of wine and 2 glasses. She sat on one of the couches and patted it a few times, "Come, boy and sit with me, talk to me." She took the paper and pen from her bag and talked softly to Jacinto. "Your mother will miss you if they take you away and believe or not, so will your father. Face the fate like a man. It will not be bad like you think and it will be all done. You write to your parents a nice note that they will find tomorrow. Tell them you gonna miss them but it will not be long you are again together. They will find it when they are back after court tomorrow and they will be better. If they do not take you away, they will be happy too. Here have a glass of wine and Mama has sweets close I know. Get some and I will hold your hand for a little before I leave if you like." Jacinto stopped sobbing long enough to take a large gulp of wine and he wiped his mouth with the back of his hand. "Go get some tissues and splash some water on your face," Maria whispered in Portuguese then refilled his glass with a little more wine. Jacinto slumped onto the couch beside Maria. "No one knows if ICE will even take you from the court. It is only for sentence. The judge might be happy tomorrow. Know if you leave for jail or out of country, it is not long before you are again with family." Jacinto just nodded. "I just want to be alone for now. I will write the note for my parents." Maria carried their glasses to the sink, took a tissue from her pocket before she poured a last glass of wine for Jacinto. She dumped the rest of the wine into the sink, washed her glass and quietly went back upstairs. Julia was waiting anxiously in the kitchen. Maria calmly assured her that Jacinto was going to be ok and if he went away, they would be together again soon.

Maria cried as she walked home slowly. Gina stepped out of her front door and waved hello. Maria reached into her pocket, pulled out a wad of tissues and several small plastic bottles and dropped them in the trash at the street corner and called out "Hello, Gina. How are you today?" If you wanted news to travel quickly, you told Regina Castello and if you had a secret, you just said "How are you" to Gina and left quickly. "I must get home to tend to the roast in the oven now, but it has been nice to see you, Gina," Maria said as she walked away. Gina blotted her fresh lipstick with a tissue, walked over to the trash, looked closely and dropped her tissue before she got into her car.

The next morning the loud banging on the front door, doorbell and phone ringing at 5:30 a.m. woke Maria even before her alarm to go to Mass. She ran to the front door with her phone in her hand and her robe half covering everything she tried to cover. "Come in, come in," she shouted. Julia Borges in the front of the crowd stood looking disheveled and broken. She cried uncontrolled as Gina held her up and handed her more tissues. Two other women cried and wailed as Maria herded them into the living room. "*O que e' isto*?" (What is this?) Julia started shaking and wailing louder. "*Meu filho, meu filho*!" (My son, my son!) Maria asked, "What is wrong with Jacinto? Did he run away?" Gina could not be quiet any longer. She told how when Julia and her husband went to get Jacinto to have what probably would be their last breakfast and Mass together they found him on the couch in the basement. There was a note to his parents. He commit suicide. "Such a coward!" she added. "Enough!" Maria spit out to her.

Julia was crumpled on the couch still murmuring, "*Meu filho*." "Things to do," Maria told the group. She asked if the police were called, yes they said. She asked if the court was called and everyone looked at her. She shook her head, of course they did not want police coming to the house to look for him for court and upset Julia and her husband. She helped Julia off the couch and told her they would go with her to her house. The band of mourning women bustled to Julia's house. Neighbors going to their cars to go to work saw the odd group and women rushed over to kiss Julia and tried to comfort her. It was obvious that Gina had been heating up her phone early this morning. Antonio sat at the dining table staring at nothing. The police were still in the basement and Jacinto still lay on the couch, covered with a sheet and the stretcher waited to take him away. Julia was allowed to say goodbye to her son. She turned down the sheet that covered his face and kissed his cold forehead. She was not crying anymore. She stroked his thick, dark curls. The officer who was putting things into plastic bags, placed the note into a bag and told Julia they would give it back to her soon. After they took Jacinto away, Maria walked the few blocks to the church rectory. She needed to talk to Father Avila.

IV

Maria entered through the kitchen. The housekeeper, Gloria was sitting at the kitchen table with a cup of coffee. Maria could smell the cigarette smoke and saw the dishes sitting in the sink. "Hello, Gloria," she said cheerfully as she took her cup, dumped the coffee in the sink and opened the window. She reached under the sink, took the whiskey bottle and dumped it down the drain. "The kitchen will be spotless when I am back after I see Father Avila." Gloria tried to tell her that Father Avila was just getting dressed to go serve Mass, but Maria never heard and did not care. She went up the stairs. This rectory was 100 years old and could be magnificent place if it were taken care of, she thought. There at the landing the door to Father Avila's room was open and Maria saw Sergio Avila in a suit she had never seen on him... his birthday suit. It could use ironing, she giggled to herself and coughed. Sergio turned and faced Maria. He was unruffled and through his bloodshot eyes he could not help but smirk hoping that he had embarrassed Maria, but he had not.

"Dress for Mass and listen," Maria ordered. "Jacinto Borges commit suicide this morning. You give him a *Catolico* (Catholic) funeral." Sergio thought only for a second to object, but continued to get dressed. As they walked out of his room, Maria looked over the railing and saw Gloria looking up at them. "Gloria, rail is sticky. After you wash kitchen floor, it will be very nice to clean all woodwork." Maria walked quickly through the kitchen and out across the schoolyard back to the Borges home. The women were still drinking coffee and crying and Antonio and some of his friends were standing around under the grape arbor in the backyard. Cars were starting to pull up and women were walking into the house with platters and pans of food. Men were walking into the back with cases of beer and jugs of wine. Maria walked into the house where Julia stood like a zombie in the doorway to the pantry, a chubby, Portuguese zombie. Her puffy, hazel eyes were bloodshot and her hair looked like she had not combed it, which she had not. Maria excused herself and went out onto the front porch to use her phone. Gina walked up to the porch. Maria noticed her outfit of linen slacks and silk flowered top and perfect makeup so she knew Gina had gone home to change. Gina was divorced and not a widow so she never wore black.

They went into the house and Maria set out all the pastries and breads people kept bringing. She made pots of coffee and washed coffee cups and saucers and set them back out. It wasn't long before the doorbell rang. Everyone stopped because no one rang the bell, friends just knocked and entered. It was Steph the hairdresser from up the street. Maria found Julia sitting on the couch in the basement. She told her that she had called Steph to fix her hair and while they did that, Maria was going to run home to change and then she would pick out something for Julia to wear. She gave Julia a hug, a kiss on each cheek and whispered into her hear, *"Forca, mulher,* (be strong, woman). She would have offered to bring something from her own closet, but she did not have time to shorten any of her skirts or dresses. She did have a few black blouses that she could set aside to give Julia. She would be wearing black to mourn her son for a year.

The day went by with the friends and neighbors, gossips and the curious coming in and out. Early in the evening, the doorbell rang. Even acquaintances only knocked, the doorbell was for priests, strangers and police. It was a police officer. Antonio was already drunk and when he saw him, in his broken English, he shouted, "He is gone, you cannot come here to arrest my baby boy," he shouted. Officer Castro stood stoiclly listening to the rant. Quietly he asked if he could speak to Antonio and Julia together.

There were people everywhere. Antonio shooed everyone out of the pantry and brought the officer there. Antonio's eyes were so bloodshot, Nelson Castro could hardly tell what color his eyes were and the sweat soaked his shirt, he was disheveled and unsteady, but he hoped what he told the couple would be some comfort. Antonio said, "You can't be a Portuguese boy, you are so tall." Julia shredded her handful of tissues and cried quietly. Nelson just wanted them to focus on what he had to tell them. "Your son did not commit suicide, he died of a heart attack. The three of them just stared at each other for a moment. Julia laughed as the news sunk in. She laughed even more and said, "Thank you, God!" Nelson tried not to be surprised at anything people said or did, but this had him a little confused. Maria was standing guard not far away and rushed in when she heard Julia laugh. She was more than surprised to see Antonio with his face buried in Officer Castro's chest. His sobs were so loud that mourners gathered to watch. Nelson stood at attention, but he slowly put one hand on Antonio's shoulder until Maria came and pried him off.

The next few days came and went as they do for any sad event, a blur of activity with some scenes etched in your memory and the rest unrecognizable behind the tears. Maria silently cleaned, organized, soothed the situations. When the house was suffocatingly full of people and the yard was full of cigarette smoke, beer and wine, she brought the children who accumulated to the nearby park where they could run and screech and she set up gallons of ice cream on the nearby picnic tables that the children devoured. In a week or so life went back to normal for most of the neighborhood. One day when she was on her way into Julia's house Antonio pulled her aside. He was thanking Maria for all the attention she had given them and took a handful of money from his pocket. "I know you must need help, no husband but still bills to pay." He was stumbling over the words and tears were welling in his eyes. Maria took his hands, "Give this to Father Avila. Para a alma do Jacinto." (*for Jacinto's soul*)

V

Now it was June and Maria needed to start refilling her freezer. She had a small hutch in her yard for a few rabbits. It was time to bring some of the young ones to the butcher who would slaughter and dress them for her in the basement of his shop. It was not that she didn't have the heart to do that, she just did not have the time. There were so many people who needed babysitting for them to be able to go to work, so many people who were sick or dying, so many people who needed help.

On one rainy day at about 9 a.m., Gina stopped by Maria's house. Gina had knocked and walked in as was their custom and there was Maria up on the ladder dusting the top of the doorframes in the dining room. "Sorry to interrupt, Maria, but I came by to give you some news and warn you about some mischief that is happening in our area. Maria came down from the ladder, pulled the kerchief off her head, the apron off and draped them on the ladder. "I will wash my hands then make some coffee for us or do you want tea?" Gina answered, "I am not sick." Maria smiled as she washed her hands, she knew Gina must have a lot of gossip if she planned to stay for a cup of coffee. "There are gangs coming into our neighborhood. They mostly were down at the docks and they hang out in other parts of the city like the avenue, but they have been seen at Ashley Park." Maria rolled her eyes as she got the coffee pot, but Gina did not notice. "Gina, there is always these things in the city, drive-ins and bangs, but our neighborhood is safe." "It is called a drive-by and the bad boys are gang bangers and it is in our neighborhood. Now they are not just coming from Providence, but Boston and New York too. This neighborhood is getting older and there are newcomers coming in that have no respect for the old ways."

Maria knew this to be true, but she did not need Gina to run to their old friends yelling "Fire," so she just acted like this was new news. Maria had noticed more spray painted signs and broken windows on the empty stores. She even had suspected someone had tried to break into the shed she had in the backyard, but she was not sure. "We can have a meeting of the *Irmandade do Espirito Santo* (Sisterhood of the

Holy Spirit) tomorrow after 9 a.m. Mass. Julia is not to her work since Jacinto died and Nelia and Suzanna retired. You can call the *irmas* (sisters) to ask them to meet." Thirty years ago there were a few dozen women who met to organize and work the church's festas and find ways to raise money for the church, for scholarships, and even bake breads and patries for sales, but now there were only 5 of them left.

So, the meeting happened the next day. The door to the Sisterhood hall was left open. At 9:15 with coffee made and papers and pens available for notes Maria began trying to convince these ladies that they must try to find some way to unite this neighborhood. Their little festivals were not intersting to the newcomers to the neighborhood. They didn't have to be Catholics or Portuguese to hold these few blocks together. She looked up.

No one had closed the door and there was a young lady standing in the doorway. "I was curious about what was happening in this building. It never seems there is anyone ever here and there are no windows and the door has iron bars. What kind of place is this?" "Irmandade do Espirito Santo," Maria said as loud as she could. "Don't know what that means.... is it some kind of secret club?" Gina spoke perfect English, so she stood up and spoke up, "We do work for the church. Are you Portuguese or at least Catholic?" Gina smoothed out her skirt and sat again. "No, I am American and I don't go to church. That's what my grandparents do." Maria tried to smooth out the situation. "The *festas* at Mt. Carmel is all very nice. We will have one soon and you will come?" "Yeah, maybe," Tiffany turned and left.

Gina shot out of her seat and slammed the door shut. "Did you see all that cheap jewelry halfway up her arm? The makeup and when she whipped her ponytail I know I saw a tattoo on her neck." Nelia swallowed her coffee so fast, she almost choked. She wiped her lips with the tissue that was wrapped in her chubby hand and spoke , "Did you see she had a baby in a carriage out there? And why is she walking around and not at work?" She left her seat to throw her cup and tissue in the trash as Maria addressed them all. "If she does not make trouble for our streets, we do not care what she looks like."

Their "meeting" continued. Even though there was no festival planned, they decided that some sort of block party could get neighbors to meet each other. They could ask their grandchildren about music and food that would attract the younger people and decorate their fences and front porches to make it festive. The park is only a block away and after a baseball game, there were plenty of parents and kids around. Maria took more mental than written notes, but she knew already how it would work out. They continued plans as they would for any party and in an hour they had the final plans.

Maria and her crew of Portuguese "sisters" talked to neighbors and their kids . They cooked and decorated. Every porch and front fence was decorated. There were banners from the light poles and for 2 blocks the streets looked like a party. Every home they went to had agreed to help in some way since it was for Madrinha. Gina carried flyers in her designer bag and had neighborhood kids tack them to telephone poles, Connie decorated her husband's wheelchair. They looked like a float from a parade with streamers waving behind his chair as they gathered supplies from local shops. Skinny little Manny was buried in bags as they wheeled to the Sisterhood. Even Julia quietly helped. She stenciled the small signs that Gina had written to place around the ballfield at the park.

It seemed like the perfect day for a party. Not too hot, but the sun brightened everything. Kids selling lemonade and drinks at the street corners had set up. The baseball games had started early and the kids and parents were wandering over to the party streets and tried all the sweets and other foods. Some of the neighbors had small crafts that they had made set up for sale. The neighborhood party was going well. People were talking and kids were enjoying the day well into the afternoon.

There were young men riding their bikes back and forth from the park. Maria had never seen them in the neighborhood. Gina came over, the heels of her lucite sandals clacking on the sidewalk. Maria was setting out a fresh platter of cookies wrapped 2 in each package when Gina grabbed her by the elbow and pulled her aside. One of the neigbors had a ring toss game and the 3 bike riding young men sat on their bikes lighting cigarettes and watching.

"Look at them," Gina said, "they are not from our neigborhood and they are not boys either. From my kitchen window I can see the baseball field and they ride around there when there are no games late at night. They are up to no good." Maria nodded, "Go check on the other booths before you go back to your house. No one is watching your stand?" "Malasadas all sold out and the strawberries in yogurt with crushed almonds are almost gone too. Besides my niece is there. You know her, my brother Flavio's girl. She is cute and is playing the music on her phone that the kids like. They are buying the sweets just to come to talk to her. My booth is always a hit." "Go anyway," Maria said. She waited until Gina was around the corner and she approached the 3 boys. When she got closer she could see that they certainly not were boys, and the look in their eyes was ?.. arrogance?

"Do you men want to make a few dollars? I need help in half hour to take these tables into the back yard. You look strong enough." One punk flipped his cigarette in her direction, but he was stopped by his friend. The friend flashed his fake smile and said they would be back. Smiley told his punk friend to pick up the cigarette butt. "Where am I supposed to put it?" he said, but his voice trailed off with one look from the charming one. He shrugged and popped a wheelie and rode off quickly toward the park.

Maria put all her food away. As she walked by neigbors' houses, she told everyone the party was over and they should put things away. The next house she stopped at was Julia's. Julia did not set up anything for the "party" but she did wear her best black dress and decorate her front porch. She had put Jacinto's radio on the porch playing his favorite cd's. This was progress, Maria thought. It certainly was better for Jacinto than being deported and off to jail. She went into the back yard where Julia sat at the picnic table under the grape arbor. She was crocheting something very lacey, and she did not notice Maria walk over to her. Julia's grey hair was now silvery white and she looked even smaller than she did weeks ago. "Julia, how are you?" It took Julia a few moments to slowly turn and face Maria. The sadness that Maria had seen in Julia's eyes seemed to have changed. Was it anger?, Maria thought. No, it was a resolve, then Julia spoke, " I am all done with this. My son is gone and I know he is safe and always in my heart, but I have two other sons and a husband who need me. These drugs that gave Jacinto this misery must go." She stood up quickly and now appeared to be even taller that she was. This was good and Maria knew Julia would be fine, but the issue at hand was getting everyone off the streets. "Take down your decorations and bring in Jacinto's music. We are closing down our streets for now."

The only sounds in the neighborhood now were of tables being dragged back into the yards. People were pulling down the streamers. Gina had an army of young boys pulling the posters off the telephone poles and soon the sidewalks were swept clean of any sign of a party. Maria had a comfortable chair on her front porch and she sat there with a glass of wine. She lit a cheroot as was her Sunday evening routine. She waited. Twilight brought the streetlights... and the 3 arrogant bike riders from earlier. She knew they would be back and she knew it would be when no one was around. "Hey, lady, you said we could make a few bucks if we helped you. There are only two tables here, how much money you givin' for this?"

Maria put out her cheroot to save for later and pulled two $5 bills from her pocket. She stood at the top of the porch steps looking down and they leaned on the handlebars of their bmx bikes like they were Marlon Brando on his motorcycle in the Wild One, but then Maria had never heard of Marlon Brando and these punks only had seen posters of The Godfather fading away on the walls of the garage where they hid stolen car parts. "What the.... ? We came all the way back here to split ten bucks?" the punk turned to Smiley. "You said it would be worth it to come back. I'll see you later." The third of the trio turned his bike to follow and they sped away leaving Maria with money in hand waiting for the smiling punk to respond. She knew this would happen and she knew what was coming.

They folded the two tables and Maria helped carry them into her back yard although she knew all along that she could do it herself. "What is your name, young man?" she asked. "Do you ever pray?" "Eddie, just call me Eddie. And what do I call you?" he said quietly. "You may call me Madrinha. That is godmother and everyone knows I help everyone." He knew something was up. He was trying to figure out how to stay on Maria's good side because he also knew that if he could control Maria, there would be this whole little Portugal for them to rule without anyone asking any questions. She was the key. He could play the part of a good boy for a while. "Yes, I pray," he answered softly, "but my friends don't know about it. I know you help out Father Avila at Mt. Carmel a lot. Do you think I could help too?" He put on his sweetest face that did not fool Maria in the least. "I do have something to do at the rectory for Father Avila if you would like to help with that." "Tonight?" "Yes, I need something done so the good father can have it by the time he says his first Mass in the morning." "I guess, alright." He had forgotten to use his tough-guy attitude, but it still did not sway Maria's opinion of him. She knew who he was.

"Do you know the church yard at all? The yard between the church and the auditorium? Behind the church near the basement door there is a metal locker. I understand that one of the boys dropped it in there instead of the garden shed and Father Avila could not lift it out. It will take only a moment, but it will be a nice surprise for him." Ed shrugged his shoulders. It was a small price to pay to win Maria, and maybe Father Avila, over. It would not take that long because he still had to meet his two 'employees' to tally up the day's sales. It was just pot and pills today since the next shipment of C and horse had been scooped up in that raid on Beetle Street.

"I will walk over and you can wait for me there. I need to get the key in the rectory," Maria told him. Eddie had time for one ride around the park to check how many customers were waiting. The park was only a quarter mile around and he would be there before Maria could get her fat ass to the church yard he figured. Maria put her husband's old sweatshirt and his old sweatpants on over her dress, quickly stashed what she needed into the huge pockets and out the door. She walked quickly, but walked north instead of south, walked down Thompson and down 4 blocks to Crapo Street, then south making a giant unnecessary loop. When she came up Katherine Street she saw the park through the parking lot for the shops. It seemed that Eddie had time to meet up with one of his customers. This was good for her plan. She breathlessly let herself into the side door or the rectory. She knew that Father Avila was too cheap to put any security cameras near the rectory, church, auditorium or school, although he told everyone that it was because he was too trusting. It was only 8 p.m., but she knew Father Avila was up in his room asleep with the tv on and his bottle of whiskey and glass on the table beside his chair.

Eddie rode his bike down the stairs beside the church to the paved church yard. Maria was glad he did not get hurt because she did not know how she would explain her presence here to an ambulance. He would not have found her if he did not know where the locker was already. It was painted black and he often met clients here who did not want to be spotted out in the open at the park especially if they wanted to use as soon as they bought whatever they bought. They could hide beside the locker and zone out for a half hour here before moving on. Whatever, Eddie thought, as long as they paid they could do whatever they wanted.

"Whoa, what is this getup you got on?" Ed remarked. Maria looked like an old Portuguese ninja in the outfit she had on over her clothes. "I get cold at this time of night," Maria explained. Ed didn't care even though it was almost 70 degrees out. "Will you pray with me?" Maria asked softly. "PRAY? You crazy? I am just getting this shed open for you, not going to church! You pray!" Ed stood up to leave. "I will pray quickly, you listen, Lord, God, Jesus, we beg you to keep us safe. Keep Eddie far from the evilness of this world until he is safely in your arms. Now here are the keys," Maria handed a set of keys to Eddie. "There is one lock near the bottom of the door and you might need to kneel and try the keys. I don't know which one it is." Ed would be glad to be rid of this strange old bitch and he was glad he had already met one customer to get him to his goal for tonight was 1k profit since it was a short night. Maria took the facecloth that she had taken from the stack in the linen closet in the rectory. Eddie was frantically trying every key on the huge ring Maria had handed him. He did not notice Maria spray the facecloth with the can from her pocket. He smelled something for a second as Maria quickly and firmly held the cloth against his nose and mouth. His eyes closed and she lowered him to the ground. She took the syringes from a pocket and injected Ed's arm, then pulled the sleeve of his other arm and injected that too. Then she went back to the first arm and for good measure she injected that arm again. She used all three syringes.

Maria slipped her hand into Ed's pocket and took several $20 bills, but she replaced the rest of the wad. All she wanted was something to give Father Avila for a few Masses. She patted Ed's head and gave a kiss on his forehead, then stood up. Quickly she put everything back into her pockets, went by the rectory side door where she dropped the keys on the table and left as she had come.

On her brisk walk home she stopped to tie her sneaker. She took a moment to break the points off the syringes, drop them to the ground, crush them under her heel, and kick the shards down the sewer. It took only a few more minutes to get close to home. Maria went one block up from her house and took a path between the three decker houses that had no fence to her own backyard. She had brought no ID or keys with her, so she went into her greenhouse. She took a small tin out of the bag of manure and took the house key from it. She went into the house and put the sweatshirt and pants and all the clothes including the sneakers she was wearing into the washer, put soap and half a bottle of hydrogen peroxide into the water and started it. She walked through the house naked and went up to bed.

VI

Every Sunday in almost every house in the neighborhood families bustled around getting ready for church and this Sunday was not different. No bustling in Maria's house, though. She always had her church clothes chosen and ready, pressed and hanging on her bedroom door. It was not hard to pick either a black dress or black blouse and skirt so it never took long for Maria to get showered and dressed. Just as she was going out the door, she noticed the red light blinking on the answering machine. She left the door open and in a step, hit the button on the answering machine. What a surprise to hear her brother's voice. "Maria, it's Augusto. I told you last week that I would try to bring the family to visit. We are already driving. We will see you in a day, we will stay in Lowell tonight. Call my mobile when you get the message. I already tried to call you a few times." He must have called while she was out last night. If Gus was driving from Montreal, Maria had plenty of time. She needed to get to church.

She did not go to the chapel doors of the church as usual, but she went around to the churchyard. There were police cars and an ambulance and flashing lights everywhere. "Nelson," she said to the tall officer, "how is your mother?" Officer Nelson Castro turned to face her. "She is good, Madrinha, thank you. Just returned from her yearly trip to Portugal." "What happened here? More things stolen?" Maria said trying to look past him. "Father Avila found a body here this morning. Must be an OD." "I will pray for his soul today," Maria said as she went to the side door to go to the vestry. She stopped Father Avila just as he was going into the church. "Father, here is some money. It would probably be a great act of charity to have a small service for the person who they found dead in the churchyard. After all, it is your churchyard where he or she died." Father Avila almost gave himself whiplash by turning his head too fast. "He was doing drugs and he was desecrating the church by doing it here." Maria grabbed his shirt at his throat, "You will have a Mass for this person. You do not judge a child of God." She turned and as she walked away, "*Desgracado*, he says he is a Catholic priest." Officer Castro stepped over to Maria, "C'mon, Madrinha, they have to take the body away." He nodded toward the stretcher with the vinyl shrouded body. Maria touched his arm, "Come visit tomorrow. Tell your mother Gus will be here with his *familia* tomorrow. Maria went home and cleaned her immaculate house.

By 9a.m. the next morning they were there on her doorstep. Gus knocked as their father had always knocked on the door. *Shave and a haircut....* Maria pulled the kerchief off her head and came running from the kitchen as they spilled into the living room, Gus, his wife Iria, their two boys Nathan and Peter and their daughter Elise. "Come, come and eat," Maria herded them into the kitchen. The boys ran ahead. They knew there was enough food and treats to feed an army which was almost enough to satisfy them. They were 11 and 15, one chubby and strong and one wiry and tall. Elise walked slowly as Marie Antoinette must have done behind Napoleon on their wedding night. Gus gave his sister a big hug and lifted her from the ground. Although he was big and burly, Maria was a challenge for him to bend low enough to lift her. Maria giggled as she had as a child when he would lift and swing her around when he got home from his day's fishing trip. Iria put her hand on Gus's shoulder. "*Basta,* that is enough, I am sure there is hot coffee in the kitchen." Gus dropped Maria to her feet and she smoothed her apron. "Yes, come, eat and drink." Iria quickly walked between the brother and sister. She was as tall as her husband, very thin and although they had been in a car all yesterday afternoon and again this morning for a few hours, she looked like she had just stepped out of a magazine... Hair perfect, make up perfect, nails done perfectly and dressed perfectly. Maria tried to feel sorry for her, worrying so much about her looks and what people saw, but she usually just felt angry. Maybe she was feeling the anger for her brother who saw how shallow this woman was and still defended her and obeyed her even when it made him a fool. Maria sighed and went into the kitchen and put more water in the kettle. She made coffee for them in a French press.

Like on cue, the doorbell rang. "I'll get it," her nephew Peter sprung up from his chair. "No sit," Maria was curious. It was unusual for anyone to wait for her to answer the door, they just knocked and entered. It was Officer Castro with his mother, Maria Matilda Castro. Senora Castro was tiny and looked like she was 80 although she was only 60. She had a black kerchief covering her black hair. She carried a large black purse that looked like it carried only a handkerchief. Her dress was black and long enough to cover her from her skinny neck to her bony ankles. Her little white ankles were the only color other than black, her shoes were black too. Maria thought she looked like an exclamation point. "Come, sit. Gus, come see Senora Castro. She came here just to see you." Mrs. Castro's husband had been a great friend of Gus's when Gus fished with him. Maria left Gus with Matilda Castro and brought Nelson into the kichen to meet her sister-in-law and the children. Matilda liked seeing Gus but she always spent the first 20 minutes or so of their visits crying and telling Gus how lucky he was to leave the docks and stop fishing before it claimed his health or his life as it had for her husband Nuno and Maria's husband Jose. Gus was patient with her and as much as he loved the sea, he apprecated the confirmation that leaving was best for him, as his wife reminded him every day.

In the kitchen, Maria introduced Iria and the boys, "This is Gus's wife Iria and her sons Peter and Nathan." Elise had gone out the back door and sat under the grapevine drinking her coffee. Iria politely sat and listened to the conversation and occasionally craned her neck casually to see what Gus and Mrs. Castro were doing. She did not want Gus to get so nostalgic about the sea that he wanted to go back to fishing. He owned his own contracting business now in Canada and he was far enough from the smelly ocean not to miss it, she was sure, pretty sure. She turned to give attention to what Maria and Nelson were talking about. They were talking about someone who died yesterday at church! *Meu Deus,* she said, "someone died at church. Was it during Mass?" "No, no," Nelson interjected, " I was just telling Maria that we thought it was an overdose, but there were no drugs in his system. It appeared to be some kind of heart attack. But he was a drug dealer, so it might have been a weak heart from past drug use. He is gone, so we will just let it be." "Boys, why don't you go outside or downstairs to watch tv," Iria did not want the boys exposed to this kind of neighborhood anyway, and they were too young to learn of these things. The boys gladly went down to the basement that had a pool table, foosball table and a giant tv and they did not let on that none of this conversation shocked them. They knew of the same occurrences in their own neighborhood in Montreal.

"And how do you know of such things, Mr. Castro?" Iria asked. "Actually, it is Officer Castro and I was telling Maria because she was there yesterday and so was I." Oh, sweet relief, Iria thought as Gus came into the room escorting the frail Mrs. Castro, eyes red from crying, but smiling at Gus and her son. She was also glad their work was not out to sea. Maria offered her coffee, or tea if she preferred and she had some *biscoitos* (cookies) that she had made just this morning. "*Nao, nao, vamos p'ra casa.* I tired." Maria walked them to the door and gave a gentle hug and kiss on each cheek to Matilda (she didn't want to break her), but a nice strong hug to Nelson and a kiss on each cheek to him too. Gus followed them and gave Matilda gentle hugs and kisses also and a hug to Nelson. Iria stood in the doorway to the sunny kitchen with sunlight streaming behind her, she almost looked sweet. She waved goodbye to Matilda and Nelson. She grabbed her purse as the door shut behind them and went right for the stairs. "I am going to go change and freshen upstairs and probably lie down for a rest." Gus and Maria looked at each other with the 'what have we done now' look. Maria shrugged, "Come eat. We can talk in the kitchen." They sat and laughed and talked. They reminisced about adventures they had in the "old country" before they came to the USA, but they didn't call it the "old country", they called it home.

Gus laughed out loud. "I remember when that priest, what was his name? Father Vieira caught us roller skating around the church. We didn't even go inside and he was so angry, he said we were ... what did he say?" Maria laughed, "He called us *desgracados* and said we had no respect for the sacred place." "Yeah, but we showed him the next day," Gus laughed. "We ate all that spicey stuff and then we went over to the church and farted in the confessionals before he got there to hear confessions. Boy, was he lucky you don't light candles in there. I can still remember hearing him gagging and coughing." They laughed and laughed and Maria was so happy that they had come today.

The whole day was a festival of eating, drinking and talking. Later in the day Gus told Maria that the next day he was planning to bring his wife to Lowell to see her family and they would not be back for most of the day. Peter did not want to come and wanted to stay with Madrinha if he could. Maria said of course he could spend the day with her. The next morning almost everyone was up early. Gus and Nathan were like two colts running through the house and straight out the back door. They darted back into the kitchen, grabbed a handful of cookies and a cup of coffee each and sat out under the grapevine talking like friends. They had stayed in the basement the night before watching a soccer game and now they were retelling some of the best plays of last night's game. It was always an exciting game when Benfica played. Peter was a very good soccer player in his high school. He came down soon after, grabbed his cup of coffee and a piece of fruit and out the backdoor to join his father and brother. Maria followed them out and asked how soon they would be leaving, it was already 7:30 a.m. Gus laughed, "Are you trying to get rid of us already?" "No! I did not know if I had time to cook breakfast for everyone. You said it would be early this morning." "Have you met my wife and daughter? Early is 9 a.m. for them at least. You cannot imagine how long it will take Elise to fix her hair, and pick an outfit. Three of the suitcases that I brought upstairs were hers. But we do not usually have a big breakfast at home. Peter is always in training for his sports so he eats after he returns from the gym. Nathan and I eat real food, but Elise and Iria eat, oh, I don't know yogurt and fruit or whatever this week's fad is, maybe this week it is air." Maria refilled her coffee cup. She had been up for an hour.

VII

Before anyone got out of bed, Maria had cleaned the bathroom upstairs and put clean towels out, then cleaned the bathroom in the basement and straightened the den where they had watched the game and replenished all the snacks. There were pretzels and chips of course, but she was glad they had made the *tremosos* she had put out, too. She did not even know what Gus and Iria fed their kids. There was movement upstairs so they knew that Iria and Elise were probably getting ready for the day. "Here," Maria took a few dollar bills from her apron pocket and handed them to Peter. "You and Nathan go to the bakery up Rivet Street and get some sweet breads and whatever pastry you want. Ask your father what he wants and bring for him, too." Gus took the money from his son's hand and stuffed it into Maria's apron pocket. "Unless you hit a lottery lately, I know you cannot afford this and I can." "Maria put the bills back into Peter's hand. "*Para a alma do meu marido.* (For my husband's soul.)" She looked Gus in the eye and she knew he would not be able to say no to that. "You can take a walk with them or stay here if you would like, but I am going to cut some fruit and get some tea ready. Isn't it tea that Iria drinks in the morning?" "Where is the bakery?" Peter asked. Just as he was asking, Iria in her robe came into the room. "Where do you think you are sending my sons in this strange city?" Maria turned to speak and laughed instead. Iria had some greenish cream slathered on her face and neck. "It is three streets away. They will not get lost." "I will walk with them," Gus spoke up quickly. "We will not get lost, I promise." He herded the boys out the back door. They walked quickly around the house and out the front gate before Iria could stop them.

"I am cutting fruit and I made some tea for you. What does Elise like for breakfast?" "Coffee, black," Iria replied as she looked out the window that was over the sink. "How long does it take to walk to this bakery?" Maria sighed, "The boys just left and their father is with them. Gus lived here for years before you took him away." Although she did not intend to sound sarcastic, the comment did not escape Iria and Maria saw her purse her lips. Trying to defuse the tension, Maria held out a large mug with the label from the tea bag hanging from the side. "No," Iria said as she turned and walked back to the stairs, "I need to wash and moisturize before I eat anything. I will send Elise when she is ready."

The boys and Gus brought back the sugary booty. "How about fixing some of the *massa* like Ma used to?" "*Rabanadas!*" Maria got out the bowl and skillet and sliced the sweet bread. She soaked it in the egg batter, fried it in butter and before the slices could cool, she dusted with sugar and cinnamon. The boys put sliced fruit and some of the slices on their plates and took them outside to the table under the arbor with coffee. Gus sat with coffee and his bread and talked to Maria. "They talk about you in the bakery like you are a saint. They said your prayers are very powerful. When someone asks you to pray, the prayers are answered." They talked until they heard Iria on the stairs. "I will go check on the boys," Gus left Maria to face Iria. "Elise wants to stay also. I do not know what is in her since she became 13. She does nothing." She sipped her tea and ate a piece of a peach and half of one of the *rabanadas* while standing at the sink. Then she was done and ready to leave. She gathered up Nathan and Gus and they were gone. Finally Elise deigned to come downstairs in her pajamas. She took her cup of coffee and sat at the kitchen table without a word. Maria told her that she had plans to run some errands with her brother soon, would she please get dressed to come along? "No. I will stay." That caught Maria off guard. She had not planned on leaving Elise here alone.

Maria went down into the basement where Peter was now watching tv and asked him for some help out in back. When he was out back with Maria, he found that she had already spread newspapers on the table and had a small hatchet and a knife laid out. "I will be back." Maria went into the shed which was attached to the small greenhouse and returned with a small towel. She tucked it into her apron pocket and went to the rabbit hutch and returned with a huge rabbit. Peter looked almost frightened since he had never seen a rabbit that big and the tools on the table told their own story. "Hold him," Maria told Peter. He grabbed the rabbit by the scruff of the neck as Maria had and held his back feet together. Maria quickly whipped the towel from her pocket and covered the rabbit's face. It took only a few seconds and the rabbit was limp. "You can go see the television now," Maria shooed Peter into the house since she could already tell he was not going to do well with what she was about to do. In a short while, Maria came into the house with a bundle wrapped in a bleached towel. She placed the contents into a large roast pan, poured some oils and spices over the rabbit and placed it into the refrigerator to marinate.

Elise came into the room and spoke! "I am going to make iced coffee. Do you have skim milk?" She opened the refrigerator and slammed it shut. Her face was pale and she slowly backed to the chair.

"There is a dead baby in there." She was so pale and shaken that Maria couldn't even laugh. "A rabbit marinate for tonight." Wide eyed and close to tears, Elise whispered, "I don't eat animals, especially those that look like babies. I don't eat animals anyway." Peter was not as polite and burst into loud laughter as he walked out of the room. He found his sister's horror funnier than how gross it was to see the skinned animal in a bowl in the refrigerator. "*Basta,* it is enough. You will both get ready to leave. We are going and you are both coming with me," Maria shouted. She threw her apron onto the counter and walked deliberately to the front door. "I will wait in the car. You will not take 5 minutes to come out." This was one of the times that Maria was grateful that she did not have her own children. The brother and sister were walking slowly out of the front door when Peter sprinted to the car calling out, "Shotgun!" and dove into the front seat and pulled the car door shut with a slam. The sulky Elise dragged herself into the backseat and slammed her door also. "No more excitement," Maria said with a smirk. "You will help me this morning. I need things today and we will cook many foods tonight."

Maria drove slowly. She always drove slowly. She guided the car up toward Buttonwood Park and from there onto Route 140 and Peter and Elise lost hope of running a few short errands and returning. Elise had phone calls to make and Peter was hoping to get in a run down by the beach before the day got hot and before his parents returned. He knew his mother would not let him out of earshot unless his dad came along. Maria heard the two of them sigh almost in unison. They rode what seemed like an eternity. Maria drove along Route 6 but the teenagers were no longer even paying any attention. The two looked up when Maria pulled into a parking lot at a place named Kool Kone. "Ice cream?" she asked. "I don't dairy," Elise said. "Yes you do," Peter turned toward her in his seat. So much for her silent protest for the rabbit marinating back at Maria's house. "I guess so," Elise gave in although Maria was ignorant of the protest. She wrote their requests and hers on a slip of paper and gave it to Peter with money and sent him to the order window. Maria waited for them to finish what they had ordered and she slowly pulled out of the parking lot, but continued driving away from home. Another sigh from the passengers. They proceeded to Wareham and Maria parked the car at the curb. She handed a paper to Peter and directed him to the small hardware store that was a few doors down the street. "Give the paper and money." Peter did and returned shortly with the paper bag. "The change is in the bag," he said when he handed the bag to Maria. "Good," Maria said and they drove out of town. Back to town by Route 6, Maria stopped again. In the town of Fairhaven, there was a small auto parts store. Another note and some money and in a few minutes Peter returned to the car with a paper bag and some change. "Do you want me and Dad to check out your car for you?" Maria looked curiously at Peter. "I saw the guy put that can in the bag. It's the same stuff you got at the hardware store a few minutes ago. You know you have to be careful with that stuff. Dad uses it on the old car he is working on to start it, but he always tells me not to get too close because it is not just a starting spray. You know you can pass out if you breathe it in. It is ether." Maria started a car, "Yes, and you can make rabbits sleep when you get them ready for a meal. I use for the lawn mower. You can fix that with your father." Elise still sat quietly in the back seat every once in a while running her fingers through her hair and listened quietly to her music that she played on a small device in her hand.

When they arrived at Maria's house, Elise jumped out before Peter had a chance to open the gate to the small driveway that Maria had squeezed beside her house. Elise waited on the porch, but Maria called to her to come around to the back door. She almost knocked them over when Maria opened the back door. "I'm going to use the phone to call some friends back home, OK?" and she raced upstairs without waiting for an answer. Maria lit the oven and smirked toward Peter. "I am making chicken to eat, too." Peter asked if he could go for a run and

Elise had only come downstairs once for a large coffee, so Maria told him it was fine. She warned him to return before his parents got back. Rabbit and chicken in the oven, Maria went into the tiny sunroom off the kitchen. She took several pairs of dress pants that were hanging neatly beneath the shelves of fabric. Maria was hemming some pants for one of her customers. It would not take long since she did excellent hand sewing.

Elise came running downstairs. "Dad is on the phone for you." Maria spoke to Gus for a few minutes then hung up the kitchen phone. "I am going to call my friend again," Elise said as she walked away. "Wait, Elise, you will help in the kitchen. Use the phone later." Words Elise had never heard before. Maria pointed to a door in the kitchen, "Wash and cut 12 potatoes, put in the pan on the stove." Elise stared at Maria like a deer in the headlights. Maria gave a sigh and walked over to the kitchen cabinet, pulled open the large cork-lined drawer and placed a dozen potatoes on the counter, pulled the chef's knife from the magnet and the cutting board. Maria washed her hands then cut a potato in quarters and dropped them into the empty pan. She then placed the knife in the stunned Elise's hand and plopped a potato on the cutting board. "Put all the pieces in this pan while I sew. Use soap and wash hands first. Then you go call friends." She did not see Elise roll her eyes, but she knew she had.

Soon pants were all hemmed and pressed, Elise was on the phone in the upstairs bedroom probably complaining about her terrible fate and Peter was just walking in through the kitchen door, panting and sweaty. "There are some crude guys riding bikes back and forth in the park. They were circling the benches at the top of the park, they rode across the street when they saw me running and I thought they were going to follow me all the way here. I need a shower. Mom didn't call, did she?" "No calls from mother or father." Maria's mind was busy as Peter went up to shower. She took the pans, rice, milk and eggs out to make rice pudding. Peter went from the shower upstairs straight down to the TV in the basement. When Maria followed him down, the sports channel was already playing a rerun of a recent Benfica soccer game. She looked in the cabinets over the sink in the kitchen area and although it was well stocked, she shut the doors and told Peter she needed him to come to the store with her soon. She needed mace and cinnamon to make the rice pudding. "Sure, I've seen this game twice already." Maria called up to Elise that they would be right back but not to answer the door for anyone and locked all doors before they left. She had grabbed a paper bag in the kitchen and had put some pastries in it. Maria did not walk slowly and that suited Peter just fine. He was curious when they crossed Rivet street to walk the sidewalk along the park. It was not long before the 2 bike riders followed then circled them on their bikes. Maria stopped. She had tears in her eyes, which was an odd site for Peter. She walked up to the two punks as they blocked the sidewalk while they leaned on their handlebars. At first they thought the tears were fear, but Maria put her hand on the arm of the larger young man, "I am sad that your friend died. You all were kind to help put tables away for me. Please take these sweets. I do not have much, but for his soul, I give to you." He took the bag Maria had offered, opened it and they both ate a few of the small custards. "Yeah, thanks," with a mouth still full of pastry they both said, rode away and threw the empty bag on the ground. It lay there crumpled beside the brick walkway and benches. Maria went over and picked it up. When she did, she picked a few objects off the ground using the bag to pick them up. Peter watched, but waited until they crossed the street to ask. "You knew those guys? They are not really kids, you know. How did you know their friend was dead? Why did you pick up litter at the park? Don't city workers clean it?" Maria and Peter walked about half a block more before she spoke. "Father Avila spoke of the young man who died and who rode in the park on a bicycle with others. I gave money for Masses. All people should pick litter." "And why did you put the paper bag in your purse?" Peter stopped when he looked

Maria in the eye. "Recycle," Maria said as she continued walking. They arrived at the corner store. "Want me to go in?" Peter was ready to go into the store as he had earlier. "No," Maria walked past him into the shop, picked up what she needed. The shop owner waved her off... he never charged Maria for small things. It was a given that being nice to her could put you in good standing with whatever angels were listening at the time.

It only took a few minutes to get back to Maria's house. While Peter went in and straight to the basement TV, Maria put together the rest of the meal. Elise came downstairs as Maria cooked. "There was no more coffee in the pot. Do you have more?" Maria slid the canister across the counter, "Rinse the pot and fill with cold water. Pinch of salt on the coffee." "This all seems so old fashioned," Elise said as she slumped onto a kitchen chair. "Dad called when you left with Peter and they will be here in a couple more hours."

"Have some fruit or *rabanada*." "Coffee is fine," Elise answered until she saw the platter of *rabanadas*. "I might take one of these French toast." Maria added, "Eat, but not French, Portuguese. You will help make the sweet rice. It is almost cooked. Stir please. Use the wood spoon." She moved 2 china platters onto the counter near the stove. They spread the creamy rice onto the platters. Elise watched Maria make her design on the rice using the side of a butter knife to guide the cinnamon, "My grandmother makes a different design on her rice." "Hmmph, different for different islands or villages." Maria said as she put a spoon into Elise's hand and gave a small saucer, "Taste." Elise could already feel the weight adding to her size. "The coffee is done, have *rabanadas*." This time Elise did not resist more sugar or calories.

The smells from the house drew Gus to the front door as soon as he pulled up to his sister's house. The smells of the foods from a home long ago made Gus almost cry. He got to the dining table before everyone else. "Tell me, Maria, can I help you carry any food to the table?" Maria laughed, "Sit. Elise and Peter will help bring food." Gus shrugged as he looked across the table to his wife who was just as surprised as he. As large as it was, there was hardly enough room for all the food on the table. The extra serving dishes and desserts were on the buffet table and there was more in the kitchen if they ran out.

When the meal was over and the children departed the table, Iria half-heartedly offered to help with dishes. Gus got up, put his hand on her shoulder and solicitously told her to go rest from her tiring day, he would help his sister. Obviously relieved, Iria agreed. She needed to rest and prepare her clothes for tomorrow she said as she just about ran up the stairs. As he carried a stack of dishes into the kitchen, Gus told Maria he wanted to talk to her. He poured two glasses of wine and sat at the kichen table. "Peter told me that you had some kind of run-in at the park today?" "No, no." Then in Portuguese, she told him that she was just keeping on the good side of the new set of punks that were trying their luck at the neighborhood. "The way they were talking about you at the bakery this morning, it made me wonder, though. They were saying someone just had to mention to you that they needed help, you say a few prayers with them and it would happen. You are not helping the way our father did?" Maria pulled her chair closer to her brother and put her hand on his knee, "I pray and God hears me, that is all. I do not take money for God's work. Here, do you want one more wine now?" She offered a plate of cookies. "No, let us clean up the kitchen. And Peter said you were picking up trash?" Peter should mind his business, she thought. "Yes, at night boys sit around in the park late at night and a mess is in the morning." "But he did not see you throw anything away, you put things in your bag?" She took a cookie herself and said, "Recycle," as she took a bite. "Father Avila comes here to see you tomorrow before you go maybe. Rest now." It was not long before Gus finished the last of his glass of wine and went up to bed. Soon the boys came up from the basement and up to bed, Nathan half asleep and Peter pretty tired also. Elise was up in the bedroom on the phone as she always was. Maria washed the glasses and went up to bed also.

At 5 the next morning, Maria quietly slipped out of the kitchen door. In a short while when she returned, Gus was seated at her kichen table. "What is happening, baby sister? You were not here, so I walked over to see if you went to church. It is all locked up, but do you know what I saw? I saw a little Portuguese lady in the park and she was picking up litter around the benches and putting it in a bag." "I recycle." She handed Gus a warm paper bag. "Warm bread. Goulart Bakery. I will make coffee." She made coffee and while Gus had some warm bread with butter. "I must give the rabbits fresh water and food." Instead she went into the greenhouse and opened a glass jar wrapped in electrical tape, slipped the contents of the paper bag that she had brought back from the park into the bleach solution in the jar. The hypodermic needles jingled in the jar when she replaced it under the potting bench. She then got the rabbits fed and gave fresh water and went back into the kitchen to start breakfast for all her guests and whoever might come by to see Gus before they went back to Canada.

Before Gus packed the car to leave, Father Avila did come by for his short visit. The children respectfully greeted him as they carried their bags out to the car, then they kept busy outside as the adults talked in the house. Elise sat at the table under the grape arbor and sulked because she was cut off from her friends since the phone was in the house, Peter rode his skateboard on the walk around the house and back and forth on the sidewalk in front of the house and Nathan had spread his jacket on the small patch of grass and was lying and daydreaming about how much the clouds looked like whipped cream on an ice cream sundae. It was not long before Gus came to the back door to summon the family into the car for the drive back to Canada. It had been a short visit, but keeping Iria happy while she was away from her country club and various elite friends was a full time job. Iria enjoyed visiting her family in Lowell since it gave her a chance to flaunt her "status" in person.

All were ready, seat-belted and gearing down for a miserable ride when Maria ran out to their car. She had an insulated bag and that she delivered to the family. There were fresh Portuguese *"pops"* (rolls), sliced chicken and ham for sandwiches and plastic bags of sweets. Maria handed each with travel cups of iced coffees fixed as each liked them. Gus came around the car one last time to give his sister a bear hug and kiss on her forehead. He ran back to the open door and jumped behind the wheel. They were driving away a few seconds later.

VIII

Maria returned to her kitchen. No messages on her phone, no one at the door, all the tailoring and other sewing was done and awaiting pick up, not even a baby who needed a last minute sitter, a nice quiet day ahead. She went to the canister on her counter that read treats. She knew that meant cats or dogs, but she found it amusing to put the cookies that she made in it. She reached down under the few cookies that were left and found the plastic bag with a silver sleeve with her cheroots. She took her cup of nice strong coffee and sat out in the back under the grape arbor at the picnic table. She remembered that day a long time ago when she and her husband had just bought the house. They had borrowed more picnic tables from friends and had bought so much seafood for the day that they celebrated owning the house. They had covered the tables with newspapers and they had two huge pots on each table, one full of crabs and one of lobster. They had pans of corn and potatoes on the grills and in the house Maria kept cooking large pans of shrimp and bringing them out to the tables. There must have been 50 people. They had helped move and set up furniture all morning, one crew for each room. Maria had thought it looked like a military operation. She had never seen a real military operation, but this was how it should look, she had thought. The day before the furniture had arrived, all the wives and daughters had come in similar fashion to help clean the rooms. Ceilings, windows, walls and floors were all washed. Two days before that, the men had painted most of the walls. Some of the men had put new tile for the bathroom and kitchen floors with the same precision, one crew to each area. All those who had helped had come for the food and drink for their reward, not that they had asked for payment. Maria thought of all that as she smoked her cheroot and drank her very black, strong coffee.

Maria sighed as she got up from the table. Family was everything and those people were her family also since that week. In the kitchen, she got out a large bowl and put a meal together to bring to Connie and Manny. She had not forgotten about them, but her brother and his family's visit and a few other happenings had distracted her from the schedule that she wanted to keep. There was plenty of rabbit meat left and much of the potatoes. She got a small glass dish and made a quick salad, lettuce and a lot of onion from her small garden. Maria walked the short distance to Connie's house. She knocked and there was no answer, so she walked in. There was Connie sitting on the floor crying and Manny was in his wheelchair with some paste or something all over his face and his shirt was soaked. She put the canvas bag with food on the table, helped Connie up and sat her in a chair. Without a word she went into the bathroom, took all the towels and facecloths she could find, wet some and brought everything over to Manny. She peeled his clothes off him and washed him. In a few minutes, Connie got up and without speaking got Manny's clean dry clothes and they dressed him. Manny laughed a strange cackle and began pulling at Connie's blouse. She slapped his hand and walked away with the laundry she now had to do.

Maria brought two cups of coffee from the pantry and sat with Connie at the table. Her whole face was red. She had been crying for a while. "He acts like a bad baby sometimes," Connie said with a sob. " I do not know how I will help him if he gets worse. He cannot go to a nursing home. Even if we could afford, they will take our house." Maria sat with her back to Manny who was fidgeting with the blanket in his lap. Connie shot out of her seat and slapped Manny's hand just as he grabbed a handful of Maria's hair. "He can only use one hand, but he is very strong," Maria said as she rubbed her sore head. "Go, go outside. You walk. Go to the bakery or park. I will stay here." As soon as Connie left, Maria got to work. She turned the small tv on to entertain Manny. Cartoons kept him busy and she went into the pantry to wash dishes. From there she gathered sheets from the bed and threw everything into the washer. She made the bed and cleaned the bathroom from top to bottom. She was tempted to take down the curtains also, but it was not her house. Two hours later, the spicey smell of the reheated rabbit and potatoes greeted Connie when she came through the door. She actually smiled the first smile Maria had seen her give in months. "Sit, eat. Manny is fed." Connie looked around and sat back in her chair. Besides the food she could smell the disinfectant and all the clean smells that replaced meds and urine. "*Agradecida,* I am thankful for you. Can I do for you, anything?" "When you have money, give to the church," Maria responded as she gave Connie a hug and kiss on each cheek. "*Adeus,*" as she walked out the door, certain that she would be back tomorrow.

The first tomatoes were getting ripe in her small garden. The string beans and squash were ready also and of course the kale was always ready. In the next few days, Maria prepared the kitchen for canning. The bleached towels were re-washed and ready to spread on the counter and table. The jars were washed and boiled and cutting boards and knives were all sterilized and laid out. In the mornings Maria helped Connie with Manny and if no one called with a request for last minute child care, she picked produce from the garden. The colander sat in the sink and vegetables were washed and chopped and jars were heated and filled with blanched vegetables preparing for their fate. If children came any time during the week, they were banned from the kitchen until the end of the week when everything was washed and packed away until they were needed in another few weeks for the end harvest.

In about another hour Maria had to sign for 50 boxes of grapes that were being delivered from California. The nice young men brought and stacked them in the back of the house and Maria put newspapers and old towels on the kitchen floor so as not to track in the purple and stain the tiles. Tonight some of the men from the neighborhood would put up the canopies and bring the press and barrels from the wine room in the basement. Everything would be ready for the next couple of days of making wine again. Maria knew she had to start preparing food for the men. She had ordered several cases of beer to be delivered tonight and she would put out the tubs for the ice. Early in the morning, one of the men would pick up ice from down at Crystal Ice at the docks where they supplied ice to the fishing boats. Then by 8 a.m. they would start crushing and pressing the grapes.

The next morning at about 9a.m., the doorbell rang. No one walked in, so Maria knew it must be important or a stranger. There was Nelson Castro on her front porch. He had a casserole dish covered in foil. "My mother knew the men would be working all day and sent some *arroz duce* (sweet rice) for the men. "Come to see them." Nelson thanked Maria for a chance to visit with the old timers who were almost working hard out back, but he explained that he had a call to go to, but maybe after his shift.

There was work into making the wine, but it was more of a party for all. Of course it was work for the women. Maria was grateful there was a stairway from the back of the house right down the the basement, but she did wash the downstairs bathroom with bleach every day, the red-purple stains from grapes were everywhere. Most of the families made their own wine, but not 500 gallons as Maria did and after all she was a widow, so they should help her. Once the barrels were filled in a few days, it meant in a couple of weeks it would be time to start the moonshine. Similar work went on for the making of the moonshine. The still was small so they made a few small batches of shine. As with the wine, a large truck delivered corn and sugar into the back yard since the new still had replaced the old one in the part of the greenhouse where the glass panes were painted green. Women cooked and sent over food and came to sit in Maria's kichen gossiping and drinking wine. The men sat around the table in the back yard playing cards, drinking beer and laughing until later into the evening when everyone went home red faced and happy.

Every morning Maria had set up her home and yard for the men who were volunteering to make the alcohol for her, but by 10 a.m. every day she had been to Connie's house to help get Manny ready for the day. Some days she stayed with Manny as Connie took time to get her hair done or shop or do nothing but sit in the back yard, but it had been weeks and some of her other friends who needed her help had to figure out their lives for themselves. Then one day, a knock on her door and Julia had walked in. She had never gone back to work after her son had died. Julia was sitting quietly at Maria's kitchen table. "I need you to help me." Of course Julia could not deny this saint of the neighborhood. "What?" Maria told her about Connie needing respite and help caring for her husband. Of course that was something Julia could do. Together they walked over to Connie's house. Connie was more than happy to see Julia again and to have her come to help. When she got home, Maria had another surprise visitor, Gina.

Gina brought a small gift for Maria. "I arrived home two days ago. I went for my annual trip to Sao Miguel. It was so beautiful there ." With so much else going on Maria had forgotten that Gina spent weeks back with her family in the Acores. Maria asked if she would like coffee or tea, but no she had other gifts she wanted to drop off. By the way, she mentioned that she noticed that there were only the old men sitting in the park smoking. There were no bike riders or punks hanging out. They must have found greener pastures. "I will be off to see Julia now." But Maria told her to go to Connie's house and explained to her what she had arranged with Julia. "Good plan for both."

Maria was in her car before Gina turned the corner. There were some errands that she planned to do as soon as she could. Maria walked a few blocks to the library. She had been there a few times and had a library card. She sat at one of the two computers. She spent much of her allowed hour just looking up the newspapers from home and Montreal. The gentleman who was sitting at the other computer left and Maria moved over to the one that he had abandoned. There was still at least 15 minutes on his time and the librarian did not notice. It only took a moment to get the answer to her question. She wrote on the back of a store receipt and went home. There was one more errand to run. Although she usually frequented the small local shops, she went to the Stop & Shop. Into the pharmacy section Maria picked up a few small items and several toiletries. Back in her car, she took two small items from the bag and put them into her purse.

Back at her house, Maria read the label of one of the small items that she had in her purse. She read and re-read the warnings and uses. She compared the warnings to the information she had scribbled at the library. She was certain what she needed to do. She took our two bottles of Ensure from the grocery store bag and opened one. She emptied half out. She took one of her sharpest knives from the magnet beside the stove. Then she took the tiny bottles out of the boxes that she had been reading and cut the tops off them. It was much easier to dump their contents into the Ensure this way rather than one drop at a time. If her eyes were irritated, one drop would work, but that was not the task at hand. She shook the Ensure and put it with the full bottle into the refrigerator on the door. That was enough for today.

A customer had dropped off a dress to be hemmed and she could get that done in no time. She went to the front door and out on the porch was a decorative chest. She used it for a drop box for sewing and tailoring projects to be dropped off. There were plastic dry cleaner bags and customers could leave a garment and a note in the special mailslot. Some clients needed fittings but for regular clients Maria had measurements in her notebook specific to each person. As she walked back into the house, Maria heard Gina's sandals clipping along on the sidewalk when she got out of her car. "Woo-hoo, Maria!!" Maria held the front door open for her and in the kitchen she poured two cups of coffee. She dropped the dress in her workroom and returned to sit at the table with Gina. "What is this? Strange language?" Gina was looking at the crumpled paper that she had found on the kitchen counter. Maria took it from her hand, turned it over and pinned it onto the calendar near the door to the workroom. "Was in the pants' pocket of pants to fix." Gina said, "I wanted to let you know that I saw Julia and Connie. As I said this morning, good plan for both, but I do not know how much longer Connie can manage. My husband was telling me that soon Connie could lose the house, especially if Manny has to go to a nursing home. Thank you for the coffee. Everyone is done making their wine. I suppose they will be coming to your greenhouse to work the still so I will be here with the other wives. I will bring food, of course. I must go now. I am visiting my cousin's daughter in the hospital. She had a surgery that did not go well. My husband said she should have sued the doctor, but I know she will not." Maria leaned toward Gina as though she had a secret, "You are divorced. Your husband talks much to you?" "We had supper when I got home from my trip and he brought me up to date on what I had missed while I was away."

Maria was grateful Gina was leaving since that was all the gossip she could take for the day. She assumed Gina had a good heart. Maria washed the cups as quickly as she could since she wanted to visit Connie after Julia went home. She took a bottle of Ensure that was on the refrigerator door, wrapped it in a paper towel and put it into her bag. She walked to Connie's house and arrived there in only a few minutes. Connie was in the bathroom leaning over the bathtub washing out some of Manny's shirts and the bib that he had soiled today. "Do you want tea, Maria, or coffee?" "I will make tea for us," Maria said. She found some passion flower tea in a tin on the counter.

Cha de maracuja?" While in the kitchen, she put the bottle of Ensure from her bag in the refrigerator and took the bottle that was already there. She brought the 2 cups of tea to the table. Connie had a basin with the clothes that she had washed. Maria took it from her. "Sit, have the tea. I will put this on the line." She opened the pantry window and hung the damp clothes on the line then joined Connie for her cup of tea. In a short while Connie started to get things together for supper. Maria set up the small tray with Manny's food then held Connie's hands, "Pray with me before I go home." They said a short prayer and Maria left.

IX

The next morning, Maria was dressed by 4 a.m. She sat in her rocking chair on the front porch smoking a cheroot with her cup of espresso. The phone in the house rang. It was Gus. Not who she had expected to be calling for sure. He said he would be in town the coming weekend, but gave no other explanation other than that he was going to be alone. As she hung up the phone, it rang again. This time it was Connie who told Maria very calmly that Manny, her husband of 28 years was now dead. There was no other conversation, they just hung up the phones. Maria decided to go to see Father Avila, then she would go to Connie's house to help her clean before too many people came by to offer sympathy and food. Oh, there would be so much food, Maria thought.

Maria went through the kitchen of the rectory. There was Gloria in her regular position, seated. She jumped up when she saw that it was Maria coming through the door. Maria walked past her straight to the stairway. Gloria smiled to herself thinking she would have her revenge when Maria walked into Father Avila's rooms. The old stairs creaked and when Maria was on the last step before the landing, a blond young man came out of Father Avila's door. She would not have suspected a thing if he had not been tucking his shirt into his pants and his fly was open. Father Avila was sitting back in his big leather wing back chair, trying to appear nonchalant. Maria would not have bought his innocence even if his hair was not disheveled and his pants also undone. She ignored the obvious and stated why she had come. "When Conceicao calls to do a funeral for her husband Manuel, you will tell her that you cannot charge for the funeral, your services or the church, none of it." "But, but," Sergio stuttered. "Stop. I will pay you. Only half what you ask." Sergio Avila shot out of the chair and looked down at Maria, but she was faster than he. She slapped him in the face. "Do not question me and do not have your lovers in this rectory ever again." He raised his hand, but dropped it quickly when he saw the way she glared at him.

Gloria was still in the kitchen, but she was wiping counters. "Wipe Father's leather chair and change all sheets, please," Maria said over her shoulder as she walked out the door. Gloria knew now that Maria was not shocked or embarrased as she had hoped. Maria arrived at Connie's house just as Manny's body was being taken away. Gina was already in the house. Connie was very calm. All the windows were open. Gina explained that Connie wanted the fresh air in the house.

There were a couple of young men carrying in platters of food with their parents. Maria commandeered one to go to her car and bring in the coffee urn from the backseat. Connie was already dressed in the black dress that she had saved for the last few years waiting for this day, was explaining to everyone again what had happened this morning, "Manny did not want to eat the oatmeal. He likes chocolate Ensure. I gave it to him. In a few minutes he has heart attack. I call ambulance, but I knew he died. I called Sergio and Maria." As she spoke, a knock on the door and in came Father Avila. Maria was surprised to see him as was everyone else in the room. Connie walked through the group right over to the priest. "I called for you this morning for Manny's last rights. I wanted for you to bless my dead husband. You too busy to call me?

He is gone now. They will make him ashes soon." "No, no, he cannot be cremated. I cannot do a service for him if he is cremated. We are a Catholic church." Everyone in the room gasped, except Maria. She was at Father Avila's side before he could blink and she grasped his wrist. No one would have guessed the strength of her grip except the priest who felt his circulation stop to his hand. "I think a mistake, Father. Manny's funeral is on the day after tomorrow at Mt. Carmel Church and you will be the priest." Her voice was not much more than a whisper, but Father Avila got the message clearly. "Yes, yes, I will be doing a funeral. I think there has been a ruling that it is acceptable to have a funeral for a body that has been cremated. My mistake." Everyone seemed to sigh in unison and they all mistook the tear in his eye as sympathy or a kind emotion. "Let me get you some coffee," Maria said as she released her grip. She patted Connie on her shoulder and led Father Avila to the doorway of the pantry where she handed him a hot coffee that she accidentally splashed on his wrist as she handed it to him. He winced and looked down at Maria, but she looked him coldly in the eye. "Say hello to your friend the next time you see him, but it had better not be in the rectory." Father Avila sipped his coffee for a moment and left without speaking to the new widow again.

Maria pulled Connie aside for a moment, "I can bring Manny's clothes to the shelter tomorrow if you want. "Do you have enough black clothes?" "I need to get more. I will need a coat too for the winter, my coat is blue." As was the custom, Connie would wear black for the rest of her life. Julia went over to Connie, Maria and Gina, "I will go home now. I need to fix supper. Do you want me back here tonight?" "No, I need to pray. So many times I wanted Manny to die. I need to pray." Without a word, Julia hugged Connie extra long, then she hugged Gina and Maria and left.

The funeral was peaceful and sad. The day after the funeral Maria sent Connie and Julia to a local nursing home to give away Manny's wheeelchair. She stayed behind and straightened out the house and made more coffee and even some pots of tea and prepared glasses for the wine since there would probably be more people coming by to visit and bringing more food. The days went by and Julia continued to go to Connie's house. Maria was glad they were getting on with the business of life.

X

Even though it was cold and rainy on Sunday morning, Maria sat on her rocking chair on the porch and had her cheroot and drank her strong black coffee. She went upstairs, got dressed for church and when she came downstairs there was Gus sitting on the front porch. She had almost forgotten that Gus had said he would be here on the weekend. She laughed and Gus hugged her. "Go to church, I will wait here." Maria left for church with her curiosity itching at the back of her mind. Why would Gus come alone after he had just visited. She was too distracted when she walked over to the church to notice the damage to the side of her brother's car. Mass was over quickly. Gina waited at the back of the church for Maria. She wanted to catch her ear before anyone else did. After all, she prided herself privately as having the freshest gossip. "Maria, a minute?" Maria noticed Gina's hair was much brighter red than usual, but did not remark on it, "Yes?" "Did you hear about the mess Father Avila is in?" Maria shook her head no, but nothing would surprise her. "Do you know the new city councilor? The blond young man who came back to town after he graduated from Yale or Harvard or something?" "Yes, yes," Maria shook her head, already knowing what was going to be said next. He was at that new hotel with Father Avila. "What new hotel?" Gina clicked her tongue, "Tsk, the big one in Providence? We have to do something. Maybe say some of your magic prayers or something," she looked knowingly at Maria and gave a little wink. "Private time is not our business," Maria said, but she was sure something more had to be done about the situation. She should have been more specific to Sergio about being discreet. Well, if Gina knew, everyone did. "Pray for them," Maria said, giving a solemn look to Gina. She walked away, "*Adeus*."

When Maria got home, Gus was in the greenhouse with the men who were taking the still apart and storing it until next year. Before checking in on them, she made cups of coffee and brought it to them. The jugs were already stored away under the potting bench and in the closet where they were kept and some were in the basement wine room. In the next few days Maria would deliver some gallons to regular customers. She already had boxes decorated with birthday paper. When she delivered them, no one would suspect the boxes contained the 20 proof delivery. By this time next week, Maria would have paid off house tax and auto insurance for the year and had oil delivered into the extra large tanks for heat for the winter.

Gus saw the men off and carried the coffee cups into the kitchen just as Maria finished her sewing. "I will get a coffee for you this time," Gus offered and he pulled the chair from the table for Maria to sit. The espresso was hot and black and Maria was wary. "Tell me," she said, "What is today's problem?" "Can we take this outside? I need a cigarette." Even more worrisome to Maria if he needed to smoke. Gus did not speak right away. They sipped espresso in silence. "I don't know how to ask this. How much do you know about when Joe died?" Maria had not spoken about her late husband Joe in years, dear Jose'. He had worked on the fishing boats with Gus. No one knew how he had gone overboard, all they found was one of his gloves caught on the rail and one of his knives floating near the ship. That is all anyone knew.

Gus cleared his throat, "Hmm, When you work on the waterfront and the boats, there are all kinds of people you meet up and have to deal with." Maria still did not know what this could be leading up to so many years later. "You know Joe and I were really young at the time. We might have made some deals that were not exactly legal just to make a few extra bucks." Maria did not think Joe was a saint as long as he had never hurt anyone she was not worried. Just then, Gina appeared. They had not even heard her car pull up. "Shhh," Maria put her hand up to Gus. Whatever he was confessing or going to say, she did not need Gina hearing, "Regina, see my brother visits me again." Gina went past them right into the house. She had a small suitcase with her. Maria followed her into the house and Gina led her straight through the kitchen to the sewing room. She opened the suitcase and there was a black brocade suit. The skirt was floor length and the jacket was short, but it was beautiful and obviously expensive.

"Ok?" Maria said with a question in her voice. "I need you to make this a little shorter for me and the sleeves on the jacket too. I cannot wait for a few days. I need it for tonight and you are the only person who I would trust with something like this." "Ok," Maria said as she took the jacket and looked at the lining. It was lined in white silk. It was very well made. "Do not tell anyone, it is a designer, but I bought it as a consignment. It originally cost $900. I want to show it off tonight. There is a dinner up in Boston for the state senator and some very important politicians will be there. This is perfect, Gus being here. I want him to escort me. He can drive us in my new car. I will buy him a new suit or maybe I can rent one for him. Gus!" she called out into the kitchen where Gus was pouring himself a cup of coffee since too many espressos got the better of him these days. Gina told Gus her plan for him. Gus shook his head, "I didn't sign up for this you know." "Oh, it's not Maria's idea, it is mine." Gus rolled his eyes, "I will drive you, but I am not going to escort you." Good enough, Gina thought. He would look like a chauffeur or bodyguard. That would be great. She wondered what kind of press coverage this dinner was going to get. She could possibly meet some celebrities besides meeting all those politicians.

As soon as Gina left, Maria got to work, she reminded Gus that he had clothes upstairs in the closet that he could use to play chauffeur. "Yeah, we can talk tomorrow, but we gotta finish the conversation soon." Gus looked great when he and Gina left that evening. Just working with the fabrics of Gina's clothing made Maria envious. She had handled imported fabrics to make some of the wedding dresses and some of the special dresses for first communions and christening celebrations but none of that compared to this brocade and silk.

Gus looked the part of a chauffeur when Gina drove her Bentley to the front door to pick him up. He was ready for a good time, although he would be waiting for a few hours to drive Gina home, so he did not mind that Gina wanted to ride in the back seat. At 3 a.m. when Gus got out of Gina's car, he did not notice the red glow of Maria's cheroot as she sat on the front porch. She cleared her throat, but Gus was too intent on trying to negotiate the stairs without falling off. Maria sighed, "Go drink coffee and I will talk in the morning." She turned and went into the house mumbling something in Portuguese about men getting drunk for any occasion.

The next morning was not pleasant for Gus. Maria needed to thoroughly clean the upstairs bathroom which meant disinfectants and bleach and lots of noise and lots of smells that did not agree with Gus's hangover. When the tiles, tub, basin and toilet were sparkling and smelled like a hospital, Maria went downstairs to make an espresso. After all, it was already 7:30 a.m. Gus finally emerged like a bear. The coffee did cure most of what ailed him physically, but he still had to deal with his sister. "You crazy?" she said as clearly as she could. Gus stammered and tried to joke his way to Maria's good graces, but it was not going to work. "Gina is not married, right?" Gus finally mistakenly asked. He thought Maria was angry because he was out late with her friend. "We just had a good time and you know my wife is not the type to have a good time," Gus kept digging his hole. "Gina is a beautiful woman. She knows that I am married, but she knows what kind of wife I have. It has been a long time since I was touched like that." That was it, he had just jumped into his casket. Maria was now so angry that she could not speak. It felt as if her throat was closing up. "No, you make it worse! You come here drunk and you sleep with my friend?"

"You are upset because I was drunk? The men come here to work on your still and your wine and they drink all day." Maria stood up and slammed her hand on the table, "Not the same." "Papa hit Mama when he drank. You cannot drink." "Ok, ok, sorry. Do not yell. My head hurts." "Good!" Maria said as she walked out into the back yard. Gus took one of the beers from the refrigerator and held it to his temple. Maria came back into the house in a few minutes. She saw the beer in Gus's hand and just as she was about to say something, he spoke first, "Look, I know Papa could be a shit when he was drunk, but I don't get drunk. I have a beer or a few shots of shine with the guys, but I don't get falling down like last night. Gina asked me to stop on the way home from Boston. We had some Chinese food, but I did not like it, so I had a few drinks while she ate. She said the food at the dinner was not good. Then we took a ride om Route 3 toward the Cape and we parked and just talked." "Just?" Maria said. "Well, just at first," he added, "She listened to me and she said how she does everything alone, even travel. She just asked me to hold her. She needed a hug." Maria rolled her eyes, "Just again? Just hold? I do not like Iria, but you have family in Canada. No more about Gina. I hope you washed all your parts this morning. What do you need to talk to me about?"

Gus got up to refill his coffee, "I know you and Joe were a great pair although you were not married for very long before he, you know." "Died?" Maria interjected. "Yeah, and I know he taught you a lot of the side work stuff he did. I just helped him a little, but you two were real partners and you knew all the details and where to get supplies and all of that. You know how to make the wine, skin the rabbits, you fix broken toilets, and more. And I know that since Joe has been gone, you have been working a lot with the church and doing all the things they call you an angel for." "What, what you trying to say, Gus?" Gus turned away. "You take care of babies and sick people and give even more than you can afford and you never take a penny for yourself even though I offer to give you whatever you ask." Maria still could not understand where this was leading. "Gus?" He took a deep breath, "Maria I can't be married anymore." "No lawyers in Montreal?" Maria answered. Gus dropped onto the chair as though he was tired, so tired. "Not that easy. It will get ugly. The kids are so unhappy when she is around, all she worries about is what she looks like and how much more money I can make. I don't want Elise to be like her, she already is moody." "Gus, 13 is moody." She gave Gus a kiss on his forehead, "How to fix this?"

"When we went up to Lowell a week ago, I checked out a couple of places I used to hear about from Iria's family. Some of her family made their money the quick and easy way, if you know what I mean." "What are you talkin' about? You want Iria hurt?" They both froze and stared at each other. Gus was breathing heavily and Maria could see his pulse in the veins in his neck. His face was red. Maria pulled the dish towel from the oven handle and wiped her face, although she was not sweating. It was her turn to drop onto the chair. "Dead?" "Maybe just disappear, never come back," Gus said in a whisper, but he did not rule out death. "I saw the ladder out back near the picnic table. What do you need fixed?" Gus said changing the subject, but Maria would not allow that. "*Que* ladder? What about Iria? Leave Canada. Stay here." Gus sighed, "The kids?" "Bring them!" "Not that easy," Gus looked defeated. "Tsk, tsk," Maria clucked. "Send Iria and her sister to Portugal, a present. Be gone when she comes home."

"Ok, maybe, talk about it later. I still have a headache," Gus said as he put another cold beer can against his temple. Maria took it from his hand along with the warm can that sat on the table and put them both in the refrigerator. She took a dishtowel, ran cold water over it and threw it at her brother. Shaking her head, she walked out into the back yard while he nursed his aching head. Maria put the ladder against the house and filled a bucket with soapy water, stuck a couple of clean rags into her apron pocket and draped one over her shoulder. By the time Gus emerged from the house Maria had already washed 2 of the upstairs windows. "Hey, I could do that," Gus called up to her. "You can not even open your eyes in the sun, go get dark glasses." When Gus came back out of the house, there was Maria on the ground with the ladder beside her. He knelt beside his sister and looked closely into her eyes, "Can you understand me? Oh, Jesus Christ!" Maria slapped his face, "No say Jesus! I missed the step. The ladder fell." She was soaked in soapy water and the bucket lay beside her. "Do you want an ambulance? Don't move." Maria tried to get up and fell back down. "*Merda,* my leg hurts." As Gus ran into the house to use the phone, Gina came strolling around the corner of the house. "*Meu deus*!! Oh, my God!" She ran over to Maria. "Are you ok? I can't kneel down, but I can call the police." Maria leaned on her elbow, "Another one with God? Gus calling *ambulanca.*" But it was too late, Gina was on her cell phone and had dialed 911. Maria was tempted to try to get up again, but the pain when she even turned her foot was excruciating. Gus came back out and told them the ambulance would be here soon. "Everybody be here soon, Gina called 911. Gina why you can not kneel, you kneel in church?" "Oh, grass stains. These are expensive slacks."

Ambulance, police and half the neighborhood filled the street for at least another half hour before everything was straightened out. Maria spent the next 7 hours in the ER most of the time with Gus by her side. Officer Nelson Castro stopped by the ER also since he had heard the call on his radio. "Mama said she will help take care of you when you get home. I have another call, but I wanted to let you know." When she was being discharged later, Julia, Connie and Gina came running across the room to hug her. They had been waiting there for hours. They all told her that they would do whatever she needed until she was well. Gus helped her into the car and winked at Gina as he walked around the car to leave. The wink was not lost on Connie nor Julia who said nothing, but they nodded to each other. They said goodbyes and all left.

In the car on the way home, Gus put his hand on Maria's knee, "Sorry you are hurting but this is a good thing." Maria looked at him like he was crazy. "No, no, listen. I can tell Iria that I have to stay here and help you until you can get around. She always gives me a hard time that I am too close to you." Maria did not wait for any more excuses or explanations, "You will pay for a nice trip for Iria and her sister or her mother. Do not be cheap. Pay off house and give to her." "My house?" "Her house. Give to her."

They had to drive to the pharmacy before they went home. Gus went in while Maria stayed in the car. Maria was startled when someone knocked on the car window. It was Gloria, Father Avila's housekeeper. Maria opened the door to talk to her. "Yes?" "I didn't think I would see you. I went by your house, but the neighbors said you went to the hospital. I need a favor. I can pay you." Whatever they gave Maria for pain was wearing off, "Come tomorrow to the house." Gus got into the car with 2 bottles of water just as Gloria walked away. "C'mon, let's get you home."

Gus got Maria settled on the couch in the living room and was just about to call Iria when a knock on the kitchen door and in came Julia and Gina. Julia had 2 casserole dished of food she had made and Gina had a box of pastries from Goulart Bakery and an aluminum pan of paella that came from Antonio's restaurant. Gina covered Maria's legs with the afghan from the back of the couch, "Have some *pasteis de nata.* The sugar and egg will give energy. We can get some plates and Gus can get you a tray and you don't have to get up. Do you want paella or some *cacoila* and potatoes that Julia brought?" Still in too much pain to eat, Maria took a custard from the pastry box and asked Gus to put the food away. After Gus took the food, Gina took Julia's arm and they left, "We are praying for you." It was only a few minutes after they left that there was a soft knock on the door and Nelson Castro entered followed by his mother Maria Matilda who carried a small pan of food and a sack of fresh Portuguese bread. She did not speak, she just put her hand gently on Maria's hand and kissed her on the forehead, handed Gus the food and she and her son left. "*Adeus,* Senhora Pires," Nelson said softly as he closed the door. Maria took the oxycontin that Gus handed her from the pharmacy bag, "It is too late to call a doctor now, but in the morning I think you should see a good bone doctor." Maria nodded yes, but did not open her eyes, just waiting for the medication to ease the pain. Gus put pillows on the couch, took off her plastic boot and propped her leg up with ice packs around her leg. He put the phone on the floor by the couch and the cell phone beside it. "Call me if you need anything, even if it is just food or company. I am going out, but I won't be far." Maria did not argue as she tried to relax and let the pain leave.

Maria soon slept. Gus came in quietly later, but the couch was empty and the room was straightened. He found Maria in the kitchen. She had bandaged her leg and was heating some of the food her friends had brought. "You feeling better already? Sit down and I will fix something for you," Gus said as he filled a glass with water. "All cooked, but needed spice. Poor Julia, not good for cooking." "So your foot is better?" "No, doctor's wrong. Something broken. Doctor for bones tomorrow. Please wipe the stove and *'frigideira'*" Maria winced as she brought her plate to the table. Gus pulled out one of the chairs for her to put her foot up. Although Maria wanted to talk to Gus about how to fix his life, she was grateful that it happened when she needed him here. Soon Gus helped her up to bed. Maria did not usually dream so vividly, but her dreams offered several reasons why Gus could be back here in New Bedford, some of them were disturbing. Pain woke her in the middle of the night. She hobbled to the bathroom and noticed there was light under the door where Gus slept and she thought she could hear Gus speaking on the phone. Something to worry about another day.

Gus was up before Maria and brought a cup of hot black coffee to her before she even got up. He gave her a glass of water to take more medication, but she did not take it. "No medicine," she said when she gave him back the glass of water. "If you're not in pain yet, it will be back when you try to get downstairs. I already called the bone doctor and they will call back when the office opens. What can I do for you?" There was a basin beside the bed with bags of water that once were filled with ice. "Here, empty the bags and get more ice. I will be downstairs pretty soon." Gus dumped the bags in the toilet and went downstairs. He called from the foot of the stairs, "I am going to Crystal Ice and get a bucket of ice. Wait for me to help you downstairs." "First, the rabbits and chickens, feed now please."

When Maria heard the door shut, she put her makeshift splint back into place and bandaged it to her leg. She made her way down the stairs slowly. No sooner had she made it to the kitchen than a gentle knock on the front door and someone entered. "*Hello... quem 'e*? Who is there?" It was a total surprise for Maria when Gloria walked slowly into the kitchen. "Maria, I am so sorry you are hurt. I know we are not really friends, but I have a favor to ask of you. First, can I do anything for you?" Maria took her up on her offer, "In my bedroom the coffee cup and glass of water, *por favor.*" When Gloria came back into the kitchen, Maria was on the phone with the doctor's office. She put the cup and glass in the sink and she saw Gus walking through the back yard toward the kitchen door. "Look, Maria, I will come back when you are a little better. I just remembered something I have to do for Father Avila." She left out the front door as Gus came in through the back door.

"Doctor Diogo office called. I need to go now." It was early afternoon when they came back to Maria's house. She checked messages on her machine when she walked into the living room. There was Gina, the first message of course and Julia and Connie and then one message that was hardly audible. She listened a second time and it was Maria Matilda telling Maria that she could come anytime to nurse her back to health. The last call was Iria, speaking English very clearly, "Do you have any idea where my husband is? The children have been asking me when he will be back." Maria looked over to Gus. "You did not call?"

"Well, no, I tried once, but we were so busy yesterday." "You did not leave message?" Maria asked as she handed Gus the phone. "Call now."

XI

Gus was on the phone when Maria came in on her crutches from the living room, "I know it has been two days, but it is going to be a lot longer. The hospital was wrong and my sister has a broken ankle and two broken bones in her foot. She can't even walk. No, she does not need to go to a rehab hospital, but she should not be alone. I will call you tomorrow." Maria went over to the cupboard to get a glass, filled it with wine and could not figure how to carry it to the table with crutches, "Gus, *pega la,* take this to the table. You will tell your wife you are not coming home if you are leaving her or you will go home. I am not escape goat." Gus started laughing, "Scapegoat, Maria, scape." "Ya, go then we talk about why you are here for really." Maria hobbled out of the kitchen into her workroom. She heard Gus dial the phone and then talking, but she could not hear what the conversation was, at least there was no yelling or pleading as far as she could tell. "I'm off the phone now," Gus called out. Maria put aside the dress that she was hemming, adjusted the crutches and came back into the kitchen to find teary-eyed Gus sitting at the kitchen table. She went over to him and planted a kiss on the top of his head. "Divorce?" "No, she said she will not let me see the kids. She is coming down to Lowell in a couple of days. She said I can meet her there. She is going to fly into Boston. I really wish I had paid more attention to Pa and how he did what he did. Even your husband Joe when we worked together told me about all the stuff he knew how to do." Maria did not appear to know what he meant, but she nodded her head as though she did. "What do you want to happen with Iria? Stay with her?" "No, I can't. I am so happy without her here. But I need my children." Maria hoped Gus would tread lightly, Iria was certainly shallow, but some of her family was definitely evil.

Maria started her conversation in English, "Augusto, please, *por favor*, only talk after I talk." She spoke slowly and carefully in Portuguese. She told him not to make any rash decisions or judgements. She said she knew that Iria took drugs. "Drugs? No! Why do you say that?" "I said for you not to talk while I talk." She took a bottle from her pocket. She told Gus to meet with Iria as he was planning, but he should find a way to put this bottle back into her purse. Maria said she had found it under the bed in the room they had when they stayed with her. "This is just her diet pills. I will just give it to her." " I find something else in the bureau drawer." She took three little blue pills from her pocket. "This is vagina pills?" Gus started laughing. He laughed so hard he almost choked. "You mean Viagra? Those might be mine." "Sure, who else? So what the vagina pills for ?" "Viagra! Viagra! I thought they might help with Iria, but nothing. Well, they did not help with Iria but they do work." Maria did not want to hear any more about blue pills. Gus took them from her hand and put them quickly into his pocket.

"You know I still have friends down at the docks. They remember me and Joe when we worked down there. I go down for a beer with them when I come to New Bedford. I went to talk to them yesterday. Some of them can help me. I don't need to get a divorce. I can keep the kids, too." Maria raised one eyebrow and looked at Gus. "No. I know what your friends do, so many of them in jail or dead now. You will be too if you do what I think you want to do."

There was silence for several minutes and Maria was getting tired standing on the crutches. She sat across from Gus. "Make coffee, *por favor*." Gus made a fresh pot of coffee. When he was at the sink, he noticed the ladder still on the ground. "I am going to finish the windows for you. Maria would have objected because she knew Gus would not be able to wash them as completely as she could, but she agreed.

Gus went out back and Maria went to sit on the front porch. She opened the front door and struggled to balance on the crutches to shut the door. "*Merda,* " she mumbled. She threw the crutches down and just sat on the rocking chair. The doctors had told her "no weight bearing", but it would heal no matter what she did. Maria did not realize until after she lit the cheroot that Gloria was sitting on the front steps. "Gloria?" Gloria stood up, "I am sorry, Maria. I know you don't feel too good yet, but this is important and I need to talk to you." Maria did not hide her cheroot.

"I know, Maria, that everyone around here thinks you do some kind of magic. People think you just have to pray over something and it will happen. But I have been listening to rumors and paying attention to what happens around you and I don't think your halo is on straight." The hair stood up on the back of Maria's neck, but she just took a drag from her cheroot and nodded. "Look," Gloria continued, "I don't want to make an enemy of you, I know you don't like me much, but this is a compliment. You have been good enough to get away with this for years. I heard your husband and brother and even your father had the same talent as you. I know you don't use baseball bats or guns or car accidents. I don't know how to do what you do, but I count at least a dozen that I have heard about. Since I moved here there's Julia's boy and that drug dealer behind the church. You see, that kid at the church was selling to me. Now his boss is after me to get rid of what he bought plus what my friends got. He thinks I killed him to take over his customers. I need him gone. How much?" Maria listened without saying a word, "Thank you for asking if I am ok. You can go now." She did not wait for Gloria to leave, she picked up her crutches and went into the house.

Maria had heard the phone ring when she was outside so she checked her answering machine. She was listening to the message from Claudia who owned the dress shop on Rivet Street. There was a big wedding to prepare for and she needed Maria to help alter at least 6 of the bridesmaids dresses. Before Maria could call Claudia, Gus came into the room. He took the phone from Maria's hand and hung it up. "I heard Gloria talking to you outside." His voice got louder, "You have been killing people for years and you have the nerve to tell me to negotiate with Iria? If she dies, I get the kids and keep my house and the whole business... and I won't miss her for a second. You cannot judge me." Maria was still silent and walked out of the room.

Gus followed. "What do you have to say about this?" He was even louder than before. Maria dropped onto the kitchen chair where she usually sat, but she was obviously pale. Finally Gus noticed that she had no crutches and was in pain. "What the hell?" He stood beside the table. Maria did not speak, but she did not flinch either. He was breathing heavily and Maria waited for him to calm down. "You do not learn. You will not win a fight if you are mad. There is stories all the time about Pa and Joe and you. Nobody can prove I kill anybody." Gus huffed a few more times. "You didn't say you don't do it. Do you kill people?" Maria stood and sat Gus in a chair, "Have something to eat. I am tired. Everybody knows how to kill." Maria left Gus to stew and went into her work room. She had to sit. This broken foot was very annoying. She called Claudia and then got busy with some of the small tailoring and mending jobs.

In a while Gus stood at the doorway of the workroom and knocked on the doorframe. "*Que?* What?" Maria asked impatiently. Gus stepped aside and behind him was little Maria Matilda. She stood quietly and meekly and hardly looked up until Gus left. "My son told me you are hurt. I can stay with you." The phone rang in a few minutes and it was Nelson Castro, "I am sorry to drop my mother off and run, but I just got a call. I know Gus can take care of you, but I think if my mother stays with you and she feels like she is helping, it will help her. She was found in the middle of Ashley Park yesterday and did not know her way home. She still is a good cook, though and she can wash floors and windows and do laundry, whatever you need." "OK, Nelson. Matilda can stay."

Maria thought for a minute. This might work out well. Matilda always was a good seamstress especially with hand work. Matilda could do some of the extra sewing that was coming in. "Come, we have coffee and cookies." The two women sipped coffee and ate cookies in silence for a while. Eventually Matilda started talking, although it did not make sense. "I have to get Nelson at school. I hope Joe does not make my husband again to see these bad men. They hurt him. One time he will die. You watch, Joe will die too." Maria sucked in her breath. She tried to never speak of Joe. "Matilda, I will make tea. *Maracuja,* passion flower, more cookies, too. Come to my work room." Maria used one of the canes that Gus had left around the house for her and brought Matilda to the workroom. Matilda lit up and came alive when Maria seated her at the sewing machine. There was no work to do yet, but Maria knew this was a good idea. They went into the kitchen and Matilda sat eating cookies like a kid, even licking crumbs off her fingertips. Maria left to go to the bathroom and when she returned, Matilda was just leaving out the back door. "No, no," Maria said and when Matilda turned, Maria saw that she had one of her big kitchen knives. "I saw a bad man outside. I think I have to kill him." Maria was faster than she expected to be and grabbed the knife quickly. She had run too fast and now her foot was throbbing. She said, "*Ajuda,* help me." Matilda became the meek, gentle Matilda like a switch had turned off in her head. Maria saw the care in her eyes replace the fear. Matilda took Maria's arm and helped her to a chair. "There is no one in the yard, Matilda." "Yes, yes, they know what my husband did to them and they are here to hurt me." Maria talked to her about the dresses they needed to alter in the next few days and she forgot for now about the evil men who she imagined were out to get her

XII

In a while, Nelson came to bring his mother home. Maria told him how much Matilda had been confused. He did not appear to understand. "She seems fine at home, she is just very quiet these days. Supper is always made, sometimes two or three days worth of food is cooked already. I figured that you always care for everyone else, the least I could do is have my mother help you for a while." Maria knew he did not want to believe that his mother's mind was failing.

Gus came in as they left. "We can talk now?" Maria asked. "Iria, what will you do? Do not be *loco*. You cannot hurt her. Just leave her, bring the children. Your house is paid, correct?" "Yes, just a small loan on it to put an indoor heated pool and she took a small trip through Europe." Maria took his hand, "Pay all bills today. Any money in the bank, take in cash." "It won't work. I have to get it in person and its in Montreal," Gus sighed.

"Help me down to wine room," Maria stood and took Gus' arm and pulled him up out of the chair. Once downstairs, she sent Gus back upstairs. The room was small for two people. Maria went to the far wall which was behind the small press they used. There was some decorative woodwork and what looked like 2 small wooden carved angel wings about 3 feet apart with a shelf between them. There were 4 drinking glasses on the shelf. She took the glasses off the shelf, and pulled the whole section of wall out. It opened the wall up to a small room. She was under the greenhouse. There were tap lights on the wall and insulation on the panel that Maria had removed. There was a shelf in the room and there was a stack of cookie tins. Maria brought a cookie tin out and she replaced the panel, she put the glasses back on the shelf. "Gus, come help me upstairs." She handed the cookie tin to him when he came and offered his arm. "Bring cookies upstairs. Help me to a chair. The cast *e' dificil,* difficult on stairs." They made it to the kitchen table. Maria asked for a glass of wine and Gus got himself a cup of coffee. "How much to pay off your house?" Maria pulled the cookie tin closer to herself and pulled off the duct tape that sealed the tin. "About 35 thousand," Gus said. She opened the tin and folded back the tissue paper that was inside. There were rolls and rolls of dollar bills. Maria put 17 rolls of bills in front of Gus and counted out a few more hundred dollar bills from another roll. She took the metal cookie box into her work room and came back out without it. Gus was still stunned. "Go to my bank and they will send money to the bank in Montreal and pay up the house. Gina's husband Joao is a lawyer. Take him to Montreal tomorrow. You have things at your house you need?" " I have cash that Iria does not know about and my clothes." Maria sighed, "With money you can get clothes. Iria will know you are not going back if you fill suitcase. Only get things that can carry in your pockets. Get a jacket and you put money in jacket pockets. Get pictures too. If Iria is at your house, you tell her you need jackets to keep warm here." "Gina is divorced. Why will her ex-husband help me?" Gus said as he paced. Maria smiled, "He will do what Gina says." Maria asked no more questions, she called Gina and told her it would be best if her ex-husband accompanied Gus to Montreal. They could fly out in the morning and be back by night . "Go to my bank now and send money to Canada. Pay the house."

The next morning was rainy and raw. The two men left early for the airport and Maria cleared the kitchen to set up her canning operation in the kitchen rather than in the downstairs kitchen. This was late to start her canning. Her garden was small, but she had plenty of tomatoes, kale, and peaches to can. She had already put up the green beans earlier in the summer. In a few days after the rain storms, she needed the roses trimmed and the wisteria cut back. There were messages on her answering machine from some of her friends who had small children who needed babysitting. She would call them and cancel caring for any children until further notice. There was still plenty to do.

Just as she was trying to figure out how to get the enamel pan out of the basement, there was a knock and Julia entered and behind her, Connie. They already had aprons on and took over the kitchen and spent the morning doing all the canning. When they were done, they tacked new oilcloth to cover the shelves in the wine room after they washed them down. Gina came by a few hours later and brought food that she had picked up at the Maxx's on route 6. They ate at the dining table since the hot jars were cooling on the kitchen table and counters. It was about 3p.m. when Matilda walked in and sat at the table with the ladies without speaking. Even though they were done eating, Julia made a plate and put it in front of Matilda. "I do not need to eat. I did at my home," Matilda said softly. "Eat," Maria said and put a fork in Matilda's hand. Matilda obediently ate. Maria knew Matilda had not eaten. "The jars must be cool enough to bring to the cellar," Gina reminded the ladies, "Glad we could help, Maria." But she did not stay long enough to carry any down the stairs. She brought dishes into the kitchen, rinsed them in the sink, covered the food that was left and suddenly remembered she had to meet someone in 10 minutes somewhere. Julia and Connie smirked, Maria gave a little suspicious scowl and Matilda wiped her thin lips with a napkin with no clue of what was going on. "Thank you, Gina. If you see Gus, tell him food is here." She felt so much better just giving Gina the message.

"Come, let us finish," Connie picked up the rest of the dishes. Matilda did also and began washing the dishes. When all the jars were gone, Julia and Connie left after asking if Maria needed anything else done. "Thank you, I have Matilda, but only problem is stairs." Maria walked with the ladies to the door. When she returned to the kitchen, Matilda was not there. There had not been enough time to go far, but Maria was not as fast these days. She went out the back door, but she did not see Matilda in the yard. As she turned to go back into the house, she heard a noise in the greenhouse. She slowly walked in and saw nothing at first. Maybe she was mistaken, nothing here. Then she saw a slight movement near the still at the far end of the greenhouse. Her black clothes made her a mere shadow, but Matilda was crouched behind the still and was softly crying. "Come, come wait for Nelson," Maria coaxed. Matilda stood slowly. "Is he out of school so soon?" "Yes, yes," Maria assured her. "Come, wait in the house." "Is Joe home? Nuno said they go for three days. He cannot find me," she blew her runny nose on her sleeve. "Come in. Wait for Nelson. There is no Nuno," Maria assured. Matilda stood as straight as she could after crouching and followed Maria into the house. Maria put the kettle on to make tea and put the herbs into the pot. "Nelson is coming. No Nuno," Maria assured again. Matilda looked at her like she was crazy, "Nuno dead."

Maria had some fruit and cheese that Matilda carried for her. It was getting cool out but the two ladies sat out on the porch with their tea. Nelson came and he helped his mother into the car and they left.

It was late when Gus got in. Maria was still in her workroom and Gus came to the doorway. He started to tell her of the day's events as he swayed and stuttered. "You only come from the airport?" Maria shouted. She stood and looked straight up into his face. "I had a late supper at Gina's house." "And beer? or whiskey?" Maria's face was getting redder. "Look, I got pockets full of money and I have a bag of clothes and papers in the car. Iria was not even home and the kids were at school. I know Gina was worried about today, so after I dropped Joao at his house, I stopped there to let her know besides I have her car." Gus was trying to speak clearly. Maria was already on her way into the kitchen and had started a pot of coffee. "You drink the coffee and give the money to me. The papers and pictures put on the big table until tomorrow." She knew you should not argue with a drunk, at least not while they are drunk.

XIII

The next morning Maria was ready for Gus. It was colder these mornings, but she took her expresso out on the front porch. A black Lincoln pulled up to the curb. Maria could not see who was driving since the windows were tinted very dark. The back door slowly opened and Fr. Sergio Avila stepped out. "You sit in back?" Maria called out without getting off her rocking chair. "It creates more respect and I do not drive well," Father Avila answered as he lit a cigarette. The driver stepped out from the car and stood beside the front fender. It was Father Avila's blond young man friend. He wore a white shirt and black vest, looking every bit the chauffeur. "You have not been to church in a while. Senhora Conceicao and Senhora Julia have been taking care of flowers and some other things preparing for ceremonies, but they just do a job and leave." "That is all that I do," Maria answered. "Well, there is more," Sergio looked at his feet and spoke more quietly, "It is Gloria. She has not come to work in several days." Maria sighed. "I will try to find Gloria." Father Avila turned to his "chauffeur" and snapped his fingers. "He has no name?" Maria sneered. "Todd, the gift please," he reached out his hand waiting for Todd to place what he was taking out of the car into his hand. Maria rolled her eyes. Todd hung a basket of fruits and jellies on Sergio's arm. "This is for you, thank you from the parish." That was more sentiment than Maria had seen from this priest ever but she was touched. "Thank you, Sergio." "Well, we have to go, but let me know what you can do about Gloria." And that was what Maria expected from Father Avila, he just needed to find Gloria.

When Maria went back into her kitchen, she found Gus there making a cup of coffee. "I told you no drunks in my house," Maria slapped the counter hard. "I know, I know, I was sort of celebrating though." "Celebrate inside Gina?" Maria could not stomp her foot as she would have, but Gus got the message. "You see a lawyer to get divorce. The money you gave, it is enough for what I give you yesterday?" "Yeah, I will help you put it back downstairs." "No, call Iria. Meet in Lowell. Get children soon. Now carry fruit from the porch."

In the next few days Maria went to orthopedic doctors and was able to walk without cast or boot just using a cane. Gus arranged to meet with Iria but he had to stay in Montreal for his business. Matilda was still coming to the house every morning. Together Maria and Matilda altered the dresses for the large wedding as Matilda's sewing was still excellent. Maria was getting concerned that Matilda kept talking about the giant rats living in her small greenhouse. She said she heard them at night.

Now that she was able to drive, although the doctor told her not to, Maria told Nelson not to bring his mother over, she would pick her up. Early on a Monday morning, Maria drove to the where Matilda had lived for the last 30 or so years. It was a two family house, but it was only for her and Nelson. The yard was not big, but they did have a small greenhouse that had not been used for years. Matilda was washing breakfast dishes when Maria arrived and she told her to wait in the house while she looked for evidence of rats. "*Ratos*?" Matilda turned to Maria. "*Que ratos*?" Maria told her to just wait in the house and she went quietly into the back yard. The greenhouse was half falling down with rotten wood and some of the glass was just falling out. Maria checked the padlock which was still locked, but the door frame was so rotted that she just pulled the hasp and it came right out of the wood. The hinges creaked when she pulled the door, but she could see by the overgrown grass in front of the door that she was not the first to figure this out. She wondered if Matilda wandered out here at night.

The weeds and vines growing inside and over the greenhouse kept it dark and damp, but Maria made out what looked like a ball of quilts in the back corner under the workbench. There was a smell like urine and she tried to poke the pile of rags with her cane and before she knew what was happening, it moved. It look like a big dog or something rolled around and then stood. It was a scrawny, dirty version of Gloria.

She moaned and raised a bony arm with a kitchen knife grasped in her skeleton-like hand. "Gloria??" Her glassy eyes slowly focused on Maria. "I thought you were here to kill me," Gloria croaked. She hardly had the strength to stand and she flopped back onto the pile of blankets and rags. There were brown, dead leaves in her hair and her face was so dirty she looked like she had just escaped from a grave. Maria saw food containers thrown into the corner. The sores on Gloria's face and arms and the visible needle marks on her arms told Maria Gloria's story. She was weak and appeared to be almost dead. "Father Avila asks for you." Maria pulled out a sleeping bag from the ball of blankets and shook it the best she could. She sat Gloria down since she did not think she looked strong enough to walk all the way into the house. Gloria whispered something that Maria could hardly hear and definitely did not understand. Maria also did not know how Matilda would handle the sight of the decimated Gloria.

In the house, Maria got some water and checked on Matilda. Matilda was sitting in the front room on a rocking chair. She was humming softly to herself. Maria went back out to the greenhouse. She grabbed a towel from the kitchen on the way out the back door. She kneeled the best she could beside Gloria. She wiped her forehead, hands and arms and gave her some water to drink. Gloria was even weaker now. Maria covered Gloria and went back to use the phone, called an ambulance and Nelson. She went to check on Matilda but she was not there. She looked out the windows and saw nothing. She went upstairs to Nelson's apartment but the door was locked. When she made it back down to Matilda's kitchen she heard the sirens from the ambulance. In a moment, Nelson ran into the house, "Where is my mother? What is the ambulance for? How did she get hurt?"

Maria took Nelson's arm, "Greenhouse." Nelson ran ahead and Maria followed up as soon as she could. The paramedics and Nelson were tending to Matilda when Maria caught up to them. Matilda had skinned knees and there was blood on one of her hands. Maria went past them and looked into the greenhouse. There was no one there. Nelson took Maria aside, "My mother has been talking about strange things in the greenhouse. When I got here, she was saying she had to kill the ghost in the greenhouse. I know now that her mind is gone, but I think we can take care of her at home, please. I don't want them to try to put her away." "She is going to hospital now?" Maria asked. "Yes, they want to check her out there. Would you stay with her? She seems calm when you are with her." Maria agreed to go with her own car. She would lock the house for them, but he should go with her now. "Good idea. I will go to take a report for the 911 call."

As soon as they left, Maria started searching for Gloria. There was no sign of her. The blankets and sleeping bag were folded neatly and there were no food containers. She began to wonder if she had imagined finding Gloria there, but she saw the kitchen knife that Gloria had held up to her on the workbench and she knew she had not imagined finding her. While she drove to the hospital, Maria kept trying to decipher what Gloria had whispered to her. Luckily, the ER was very busy and they had no extra staff to monitor Matilda since her injuries seemed minor. Other than a bandaged knee, Matilda was fine and they decided to discharge her. The x-rays showed no damage and the pain meds made for an early night.

Maria left when Nelson arrived to bring his mother home. While Nelson drove his mother by the pharmacy she planned to drive by their house to check the greenhouse one more time. Maria never made it to Matilda's house before she and Nelson got there.

XIV

From her purse sitting on the front seat of the car, the familiar bell of a 1950's phone rang out. Maria pulled her car over. She never could answer when it rang, but the name on the screen read Sergio. "*Ola?* Hello Sergio?" "Come to the rectory," was the only response he had.

It took only a few minutes for Maria to park her car behind Sergio's residence. She pulled her cane from behind the seat and made her way slowly from the churchyard to the rectory's kitchen door. The door only opened a few inches when she turned the handle. She pushed and leaned against the door and it gave slowly. From inside the room, Sergio Avila shouted, "Push the door open." Maria leaned on the door and slowly it continued to slide open enough for her to look inside. There was a crumpled, thin, bloody body of Gloria Torres. "*Meu Deus!* My God!" Maria squeezed into the room. "Do something," Sergio Avila held his handkerchief to his face, "Look at this mess!" "Call 9-11!" Maria shouted to him. "No, no! Fix her, fix this." "*Estupido!*" Maria pulled a kitchen chair closer to help her to get down beside Gloria's body. She definitely had to be dead. When she looked up at Sergio for a second, she thought she saw someone at the front door. Maybe the stupid priest had called for help after all, but the front door was closed and no one was there.

"Give me towels," Maria ordered Sergio. "There are only dish towels here," he answered feebly. "Give to me. Wet them." If Maria could have reached him with her cane, she would have beat him with it. He wet some towels and tossed them to her so he did not have to get too close. Maria wiped Gloria's bloody face and she was relieved that she was alive, but she must be in terrible pain. When she moved Gloria's head to wash more of her face, she saw a tooth on the floor. "Get blankets, sheets, more towels," Maria pointed to the linen closet. Sergio obeyed. "Get your car. Bring her to hospital now." "I told you no. Fix her." By chance, Maria had her cell phone in her pocket and she made some phone calls. Gloria opened her eyes, but her arm appeared to be broken and she cried out when Maria moved her. Sergio came back with blankets and sheets. "I have an appointment in my office. She will be gone soon, I hope." He was close enough now and Maria swung her cane and brought Sergio to his knees. "Go to your meeting." "This is a sacred place," he said, "This disgraceful person has desecrated it," Sergio wiped his brow with his handkerchief. Maria leaned on the chair and stood over him, "This is where you live, not the church YOU desecrate it." Sergio pulled himself up slowly and left. Maria went back to tending to Gloria.

It was only a few minutes before the two women came to the kitchen door. Julia and Connie did not ask questions, they ministered to the broken Gloria with Maria then helped her out to Maria's car. Maria finished the cleanup of the kitchen until it looked like nothing had happened there. She went over to the rectory office where she heard Sergio speaking to someone. She listened at the door for a moment then went back to her car through the kitchen. The ladies brought Gloria to Maria's house and entered through the kitchen door. She was wrapped in sheets but still looked very gray. "Basement," Maria said as she opened the door to the cellar. One step at a time and holding the railing, Maria made her way down the stairs. She spread towels on the couch by the time Julia and Connie got Gloria into the room but Gloria still had not spoken or opened her eyes. All three ladies were convinced that she was dying or dead. She did moan once in the car, but there had been no other sign she was conscious since. Maria brought a pitcher of water and a small bottle of wine to the coffee table. All three ladies bathed Gloria and wrapped her in warm blankets, but they never did find where so much blood had come from and although there had been a lot of blood on her, she did not seem to have lost a tooth. Maria wrapped some wooden spoons in towels and with an ace bandage splinted the broken arm, she told Julia and Connie to go home. Connie reminded them that she lived alone now and she should stay to watch over Gloria and Maria.

Connie drove Julia home and returned. The recliner and second couch were made up when Connie returned and the women slept. In the middle of the night, Gloria began moaning, but it soon became screaming and she was sweating and shivering. Maria made her way up to the second floor bathroom and when she came back, she gave something to Gloria and a glass of water. "More water," she said and Gloria obeyed. It was not too long before Gloria was somewhat calmed. It was a restless night for Gloria, but she still did not speak. Maria kept her eye on her. Connie helped Gloria to the bathroom during the night, but she had never witnessed withdrawal before. Gloria wretched and vomited but she was soon tired and sleepy again.

Maria made a phone call early in the morning. She called Nelson to check on his mother. She still slept, he said. Maria suggested he keep her at home to get more rest for the day. It was rainy and cold and Matilda's arthritis would probably be worse, she reminded him. She recommended he give her the medication that she had been prescribed for pain. Maria was certain she smelled coffee and went slowly up into the main kitchen. Julia was already there, she had made coffee and had breakfast ready for all. Julia asked, "Gloria is still here?" Maria laughed, "She can not run. She is sick." Julia laughed even more, "You can not run too."

They brought the food downstairs and with Connie, they all ate and had coffee. Gloria stirred. "You are not dead!" Connie remarked. Gloria moaned and was sweating and shivering, but not as much as last night. They piled more blankets on her and Maria gave her some of the strong coffee they were drinking. She added plenty of sugar and it seemed to soothe Gloria. "I bit his hand when he hit me and I hit him in the face with the pan," her voice trailed off as she curled up under the mountain of blankets.

After they ate, Maria said she had to get to the pharmacy for some things to treat Gloria. Julia offered to stay with Gloria, but Connie offered to drive her. At the corner drug store, Maria got Tylenol and a few things which she already had at home. Just before they got back to her house, Maria asked Connie to let her stop by the rectory. She said they should check how everything was since Gloria was not there to cook or clean. They went in through the kitchen, but everything looked in order. Maria told Connie to check if there was laundry piling up in the basement under the laundry chute. When Connie went downstairs, Maria went to the office. The door was closed and she could hear Sergio talking. He must be on the phone since the conversation was one-sided. "Confession will be good for you. You will be so much better soon."

Maria opened the office door slowly, but was not prepared for what she saw. Sergio was standing with his back to the door. He leaned forward over the leather couch and Maria saw Todd lying with a towel held to his face. Maria saw a bloody towel drop to the floor as Father Avila turned to face her. "Leave now," he shouted at Maria. "You need me to help," Maria shouted back. "An intruder came to steal the church's deposit money and he attacked Todd who fought him off valiantly." "Was his name Gloria? Let me help," Maria picked up the bloody towel from the floor, threw it in the trash basket and walked around the couch to face Todd. She lifted the towel that he held on his face. It was cold and wet and getting soaked in blood from his mouth. She almost laughed out loud when she saw the black eye and his very bruised jaw. The blood dripped from the corner of his mouth and Maria could see the bloody space of the missing front tooth. She grabbed his jaw and moved it back and forth while he screamed like a baby, "It is broken. Go to the hospital." Sergio brought a handful of tissues and wiped Todd's tears. "I will take him now. You must leave. Be sure that you dispose of Gloria." Sergio Avila waved Maria off. She was glad to go.

On her way out the back door, she took the wadded tissue from her pocket and when she threw it into the trash, the tooth fell to the ground. Maria usually did not litter, but she made an exception this time and left it there.

Connie was waiting in the car and without speaking they drove to Maria's house. Before they got out of the car, Connie spoke. "Maria, I think I know what happened at the rectory. Either Sergio or the police will be looking for Gloria, am I right?" "Not police business," Maria reached for the door handle. "I just wanted to tell you that you have been helpful to everyone in this neighborhood, so if you need a place for Gloria to stay, I can keep her at my house until she is better. I never liked her, but I never hated her either. You are still recovering and you have so much to do and since Manny is gone, I need more to do." "Thank you. We will see if she can move."

Back in the house, Maria found Julia and Gloria in the kitchen. Gloria still looked like death warmed over, but she was sitting at the table and drinking coffee. Maria took some hard boiled eggs from the refrigerator, put them on a saucer with a Portuguese pop and put it in front of Gloria. "Eat," she said and Gloria did. She was looking better, so Maria asked if she wanted the police. "No, no," Gloria protested. "Listen, I know none of you will even believe me and you probably don't like me, but I never wanted anyone to get hurt. I know I have been hooked on pain stuff, but it got out of hand. I was in a car accident a few years ago and that is how it started. My scripts ran out and I tried to work two jobs to get what I needed, but it was never enough so I sold pills and took some for myself. They kept giving me more and I could not keep up so I skipped town. I was living in Brockton and I thought they would not find me down here in New Bedford." "Did they find you?" Connie asked. "No, but I still needed stuff. I was getting it from that kid that died in the churchyard and I was selling a little to afford it. When he died, his supplier expected me to sell. Even if I didn't he said I owed him, so I started using more. That is why I was hiding from him, I had had enough. I was just going to go cold turkey and take my chances, I couldn't take it anymore. When you found me at Officer Castro's greenhouse, I think I was dead or almost. I crawled out before anyone could come back and I went to get one more fix. I was so sick I would have been happy if I could die."

"You went to Father Avila's house instead?" Maria asked. Gloria gave a little laugh, "I went there to get my fix." "Father Avila sells drugs!?" Maria asked, and all three ladied gasped. "No, his boyfriend, Todd. He is one of the biggest suppliers around. He keeps a big stash right in the basement of the rectory with a few guns and stuff." "No, no, no," cried Maria "this cannot be." Maria was getting flushed and she began to pace, cane and all. "Father Avila knows this?" Gloria sat up straighter, "He has no clue about anything. He just worries about looking good. He is a stupid snob. He can't even see that Todd is just using the rectory for cover, he thinks he is in love."

Gloria had more of an appetite and kept in most of the food. They gathered some boy's clothing that Maria had for her nephews. They put a hoodie and dark glasses on her and shuffled her out to Maria's car. Maria drove to the Stop and Shop parking lot and she and Gloria went into the store. In a few minutes Connie drove up in her car and went into the other entrance to the store leaving her car double parked with Julia waiting outside. Connie brought Gloria to her car and they drove away. They did not know if Todd or any of his runners or "employees" were watching the neighborhoods to find Gloria. She still owed Todd a few thousand dollars according to him. It did not matter if she did or did not, he wanted rid of her and Maria was sure that Sergio would do whatever necessary for Gloria to disappear.

XV

Maria, Connie and Julia set Gloria up at Connie's house in her finished basement. When Gloria fell asleep, the three women tried to plan what was next. Even though she did not deserve to be beaten as she had been, Connie reminded them that Gloria was a drug addict and there was no way to be sure she would not start stealing or whoring or whatever she did to earn money. Having her in the basement was alright, at least she could lock her door, but she did not want it to go on for very long. Besides, she lived alone now and she did not know if she would be safe if Todd found out where Gloria was staying. They agreed that Gloria had to move on as soon as they could.

Gloria was feeling well enough to get around better and her arm was healing well. The ladies cooked soups and herbal teas for the two patients, Maria and Gloria. For the next few days, Julia or Maria or both were always with Gloria and Connie. Every day Maria called Nelson to check on Matilda. He had taken some time off from work and was caring for his mother at home. It sounded like he was also keeping her sedated, but Maria needed to handle one situation at a time. Gloria had not left the house or even the basement for that matter, but they were sure they should move Gloria to somewhere safe soon. Maria was waiting to hear from Gus. He still had connections at the waterfront and that might be the best way to get her out of the area before anyone saw her. When Maria called his house in Quebec, Gus' daughter Elise said he would be home this evening from a business trip to New York.

Maria went back to her own house to stay for the night, she had a doctor appointment first thing in the morning. Julia went home to her husband. Connie was sure that she would be fine alone in her own house with Gloria. Maria drove them to Connie's house and made sure she locked the doors and Gloria slept early. Maria took a detour by the rectory before she went home. She sat in her car for a few minutes and watched the lights come on in the kitchen. She saw Sergio stand at the kitchen sink and just as she was ready to leave, she saw Todd come into the room. His face looked bruised and she could see something sparkle in his mouth. She had seen enough results of bar fights to know his jaw was wired. Now she could go home. When she got home, she went to the chicken coop and rabbit hutch out back to make sure Nelia and Suzanna had cared for her "livestock". They were fine and she entered the house by the kitchen.

No sooner had she switched on the light than the phone rang. "I have something for you. Can I come by?" Gina asked. Gina must have called from a cell phone because it was about a minute before she walked into Maria's kitchen. She put a box on the counter. "You must have been busy for the last few days. I have tried to call you and you never called me back," Gina said as she took a glass from the cabinet. She took one of the bottles of wine from the cupboard and filled the glass. "Much has happened," Maria said and filled her own glass. She opened the box on the counter. "This is from where? Not from Goulart Bakery." "Oh, no. I just got back from New York. That is from a very nice Italian bakery." "Hmmm, yes," Maria said and kept further comments to herself.

"Well, I just wanted to see if you are ok. I want to hear all about whatever has happened tomorrow. I am tired right now. I need to go home to bed." "I am sure you need rest," Maria answered. After Gina left, Maria called Gus again. He still was not home, Elise said, but she would have him call her soon. Maria got some bread and cheese and sat at the table with her glass of wine and the box of pastry. She ate a zeppole first then a piece of the sfogiatella and a piece of the lobster tail She poured another glass of wine and put the cheese and bread away for another time. These pastries will be perfect to finish in the morning with some coffee. She closed the box and sure enough, it read Ferrara Bakery, Mulberry Street, N.Y., N.Y.

As she slid the box onto the shelf in the refrigerator, the phone rang. Gus. "Hey, sis, what is up?" Maria was not used to hearing her brother greet her like this. "I need a favor," she said.

"Hmmm, a favor, huh? That'll cost ya," Gus slurred. "You answer in the morning when I call you," she was in no mood to argue with a drunk tonight. "Hey, call my cell. I don't know if I will be home when you call." Maria dumped the rest of her wine down the sink. She lost her appetite for now and she just wanted her own bed and some sleep. She went up to bed. She will deal with all of this tomorrow.

The next morning Maria called Connie's house. Connie answered sleepily although it was already 8 a.m. "Can I talk to Gloria?" "I will go wake her. " Half awake, Connie slipped one arm into her robe. "No Gloria here." The door to the basement was open and Connie looked toward the bathroom, but the door was open and she saw no one in the pantry. She went back to the phone, but Maria was no longer there. As soon as she heard 'noGloria', she had put her jacket on and was at the back door. She was surprised to see Gloria standing there. "Why did you leave? You are not safe. Come in the house." Maria quickly called Connie and told her that she found Gloria and told her to get ready, they were going to take a long ride later. "Sit and do not go away," Maria ordered Gloria.

She went upstairs to get dressed. When she walked out of her bathroom, Gina was standing there in the hall. "*O que e*? What?" Maria said in surprise. "Why is Gloria sleeping at your kitchen table?" Gina whispered. Maria ran the best she could down the stairs. "Gloria! Gloria! You took more drugs?" Gloria snored with her face on the kitchen table. Maria shook Gloria and she mumbled something, but Maria did not wait. She left her sleeping there, made some good strong coffee for herself and Gina. She and Gina sat at the dining table and Maria told her the plan she had just made. They would gather Connie and Julia and drive to Lowell. Gloria had family there and she could stay with them or in a shelter until she could move further away if necessary. She needed to hear from Gus. She did not have time to have him arrange to get Gloria on a fishing boat and get her up to Portsmouth in New Hampshire or somewhere in Maine, but he still might be able to help set Gloria up in Lowell since he knew the area around Iria's family.

The kitchen phone rang and Maria shook Gloria when she walked past her to pick up the phone. Gloria grunted. Maria was glad to hear Gus at the other end of the line. "You must help me." "I just have one quick job to do," Gus answered, "Then I can meet you down at your house because I need to go to New Bedford ." Maria just said ok and hung up the phone. She went back to the dining table. "Gina, Gus stay with you last night?" Gina took a big gulp of her coffee, but that still did not give her enough time to think of anything more creative than , "Yes". The phone rang before she could decide what the next step would be. Gus again. "Listen, I have to talk to you." The kitchen door opened and there stood Gus, phone still in his hand. "I have no time for you to joke with me," Maria said and turned to walk away. "No, I am serious. I need to talk to you," Gus followed.

He had not noticed Gina's car out front of the house and he just looked over to her as she sat at the dining table. Gus grabbed his sister's arm and spun her around, "It is important. I need to talk to you." Right then he seemed totally sober and he did get Maria's attention. Gus was just about to sit Maria at the table when he realized that Gloria was passed out at the kitchen table. "What is THIS?" Gus was red-faced but not drunk. He looked past Maria into the dining area and paused for a second when he looked intently at Gina. Gina picked up her purse and her coffee cup. She walked slowly and deliberately into the kitchen, put her cup and saucer in the sink, and turned to Gus. She put her hand gracefully on his shoulder and tightened her grip as she whispered in her stage whisper, "Gus just relax and do not do or say anything that will hurt you." Without even a look back, just an *"A Deus"* (good-bye) over her shoulder to Maria, she walked out.

Maria stood as tall as she could and faced Gus ready for a fight or confession or.... but Gloria stirred. She picked up her head and there was a puddle of drool on the table. Maria left Gus standing in the middle of the room. "Later," she said as she went over to the closet and returned with a spray bottle and a disposable towel. She sprayed and wiped and the smell of disinfectant and bleach immediately got Gloria's attention.

"Why you are not in Canada? What, you and Gina?" Maria spit out the questions at the same time. "Not important," Gus answered in kind. Maria squinted her eyes but she still did not see through the bs. "I have things to do. I need you to help me. I will come back in a minute," Maria left to check on Gloria who was still taking a shower. She returned to find Gus on his phone. All she heard of his conversation was, "How could I know? You did not tell me she would be in my sister's house." Maria cleared her throat and Gus shut his phone and turned quickly to see if she had heard what he was saying. Maria's expression gave Gus no clue.

"I still have clothes here. I am going upstairs to change," Gus said as he left the kitchen. When she could hear him walking upstairs, Maria went to get Gloria. She was getting dressed slowly, Maria helped her and told her that she would be keeping her here until they could find a way to bring her safely to somewhere away from New Bedford to stay, but she had to agree to stop taking the drugs. Maria asked her where she got the drugs she had taken. Gloria lied that she had some stashed right out back here in the greenhouse behind Maria's house. She had escaped Connie's house to get them and was planning on leaving town but she did not think the stuff would hit her so hard. Maria knew Gloria was in danger and she was putting Maria and her friends in danger also. She did consider that possibly Gloria should just get back onto the street and fend for herself. She was going to die, but at least Maria and her friends would not die with her. She sent Gloria to the basement to put the towels and clothing into the washer.

Gus was walking in as his phone beeped in his pocket and he stepped aside to read a text. He said goodbye quietly into the phone and turned to Maria, "Ok, what is this plan you need help with?" "Many telephone calls to you today. I need Gloria away soon. Maybe Maine or Canada. She will be here until she goes." Gus sighed, "So why. What is she hiding from? I don't need any trouble with a divorce coming up. Gina said to be very careful if I want to get the kids." "Gina? Again?" Maria filled a large mug with coffee . "Gus have coffee and *massa* (sweetbread)." Gus sat and Maria explained how some dangerous people were searching for Gloria to hurt and possibly kill her. She asked if maybe he could ask a favor from one of his friends down on the docks. Gus reminded her that these days the state pier was being watched more carefully, it wasn't the old days. Maria asked if he could check, maybe get her to Maine and from there she could get through

New Hampshire then Vermont to Canada. Possibly they could just find a place where she could spend the winter in New Hampshire or New York even. Maria was hoping that by then Gloria would be thinking for herself and go somewhere on her own. She did not even know why she was trying so hard to help her. She could have put everyone out of Gloria's misery a long time ago. Maria had never asked for help or ever told anyone what she planned to do in any situation and Gus was not reacting the way Maria had thought he would. Maybe she was just thinking of the Gus who was always so sure that he could solve any problem and always had connections to remedy any situation.

Gus agreed to try to help this addict who he said seemed unsaveable. He had to go, he had to meet his lawyer about the house he was buying in Dartmouth. He promised Maria again that he was getting money soon to repay her. He gave Maria a kiss on each cheek, grabbed another slice of the sweet bread and headed out the kitchen door. Maria sat for a few more minutes here at the kitchen table. She filled her coffee cup again and took another slice of the sweet bread. As she dunked it into her cup, she remembered that she had sent Gloria downstairs with some laundry. She shot out of her chair, went straight to the basement door and swung open the door. Gloria was standing there at the top of the stairs. "I couldn't find the laundry soap," Gloria said. That did not explain why she was just standing at the top of the stairs or why she could not immediately find a gallon of Tide that sat on top of the washer. "You can eat now?" Maria put a large coffee cup filled with black coffee on the table in front of Gloria. Gloria took one of the slices of bread, "Can I toast this?" she asked. Maria buttered the bread and dropped it in the skillet and put the jam and butter on the table. "You can sew?" Maria asked Gloria as she handed the plate with the toasted bread to Gloria. "Not really. I just get new clothes if anything needs sewing." "You will help clean. Gus will help to find a place for you." "No. I am ok. I will find a place to stay. What business is it of yours what I do or where I stay?" "Not safe for you or me. You go far away." "Yeah, I guess I should be away from here. I need to think." Maria had not even changed the curtains since she was injured, so now she could direct Gloria to help her to get back on track. As long as she could get her to stay in the house, she was certain they would be safe. Connie called to ask if she could come over. Yes, Maria told her and if Julia could come, too, that would help. It was not long before the 3 of them and Gloria were sitting at the kitchen table. They drank the strong coffee and ate more sweetbread with jam.

After an hour or so, the phone rang and it was Nelson. His mother, Maria Matilda, was missing. Could he get some help looking for her? He had left his house just to go to the store and she was gone when he returned. He already called his station and they would put out a silver alert, but by the time anyone had time to help look she could be in Fall River or worse. Of course, Maria assured. She knew it was not safe to bring Gloria out of the house. "Connie, you stay here with Gloria. We look for Matilda.

Maria sent Julia to go down Rivet Street. She reminded her to check the church and not to forget to look up the side streets and check the dress shop near County Street because they do alterations and tailoring for the owner there. It may be that she thinks she is going to pick up some work. As soon as Julia started East on Rivet, Maria went West up the street. There as stately as it always had been was the beautiful, empty former Thomas' Department Store. No matter what they did to the building, no one could take its character or that of the apartments above. Matilda had lived there when she and her husband were first married, a few years before Nelson was born. Maria knew the trick to get into the basement door. The rusted key was behind the loose shingles near the basement window as it always had been.

The cobwebs and pile of leaves did not appear to have been touched by anything but the weather, but since she was here, she decided to check anyway. The bent key eventually turned with some effort and she pushed the door open. No one had been here for many years. She knew that there had been a restaurant upstairs for a while, but obviously they had not used the basement. Just as she was about to leave, she heard voices at the far end of the room. "Did you see that old lady run?" "Yeah, she was so skinny and old I am surprised she didn't have a heart attack right there." The voices were young and loud. "What was she yelling about? Adriano! Adriano! And bangin' on the doors like that." Maria stayed quiet until the voices trailed off. She did not care what they were doing in this place, nothing good she was sure. But Matilda obviously had been here and run off.

Maria drove back to Matilda's house. "Maria Matilda Castro," Maria called out when she walked around to the back of the house. She looked in the broken windows of the greenhouse. No Matilda. It was only two more streets to her own house, maybe there. Maria pulled her car into her yard and entered the house by the back as was her custom. She went to the cellar door to check on Gloria, Connie and Julia, but she was distracted by some voices in her living room. There was Gina sitting on the couch with Matilda! Matilda was chatting like it was the old days. It sounded like she was talking about a recipe. "*Que*? What is this?" Maria said.

"Oh, I saw Matilda running through the park and I thought it would be safer here than leaving her back at her house. I did not know that you were looking for her until I got here. That Gloria person is downstairs with Julia and Connie." This seemed like a kind gesture to Maria, although out of character for Gina. She had a small towel in her lap and was wiping the smudges from Matilda's cheek and pulling leaves from her hair. Maria called Nelson immediately and he was there before Maria could prepare them a cup of tea. Gina was very solicitous to Nelson when he arrived, almost fawning. "I will be in town for a short while. I can stay with your mother when you have to work. Give Maria and the other ladies a break," Gina cooed. Maria did not recognize this Gina, but she would like the time to get Gloria settled and maybe have her hair cut and colored since the gray were outnumbering the dark very quickly. Nelson jumped at the chance to keep his mother out of the hospitals for now.

The next few days were quiet. Gloria was never alone, but she was sober and obeyed Maria's orders on how to clean the house. The ceilings were dusted with dry mop. The walls were all wiped down with a damp sponge. Every window and door frame was dusted and washed, every window was washed and left open for the fresh air and fresh curtains were ironed and hung. The floors were washed hands and knees with a scrub brush, bathroom floors with bleach and disinfectant, wood floors with white vinegar and olive oil. Maria oversaw each project and she had Gloria clean two rooms a day. Gloria was grateful for the rest when Maria went out to run errands, and left her with her favorite warden, Julia. She would let Gloria smoke outside and have a glass of wine downstairs and lie on the couch to watch TV. Connie was ok, too, but she was too scared that Gloria would relapse and kept the wine locked up. Maria was ok, too, but there was nothing warm and fuzzy about her.

Maria was getting concerned that she had not seen Gus in these few days. She called and left him another message. It was Saturday. Maria called Connie and asked if she could stay with Gloria. She came over quickly. "You have not been to Mass in weeks. Why now?" Connie asked when she arrived. "No more *Missa* on television." "You know that Father Avila says that Mass and Todd might still be at the rectory." "You stay in basement with Gloria and maybe you need this." Maria had a small wooden box that said *Biblia*. Connie wondered why she was giving her a bible. Maria opened the box, took out the small black book and opened that .. and inside there was a small black gun. Maria never used guns, but if Todd or one of his crew knew Maria was in church, they might want to check for signs of Gloria in the house. She knew that Connie could handle whatever might happen. Maria was tired of waiting for their next move and she wanted to get on with her life.

It was cold and rainy so Maria put on her black kerchief and her black coat. It was much less noticeable for her to walk to church with so many of her neighbors than if she drove her car. No boys on bicycles, but very often a small car or another with dark windows drove up or down the streets and Maria knew they were probably running errands for Todd. Maria had seen more and more of these cars driving around slowly lately. She did keep Gloria away from windows at home, but that could not go on for much longer.

Maria walked as quickly as she could manage and it took only a few minutes to get to the front steps of Mt. Carmel Church. She usually entered through the chapel and sat as close to the first pew as she could, but not today. She walked in with the families who were entering through the large front doors. Just a few years ago, there would not be one empty seat in the whole church. Maria could even remember when there would be no room to sit and the doors would be opened for those who had no seat to still attend, but that was then and this was now. Maria went straight up the main aisle with the families with children in tow. She looked like a grandmother following them and sat as close to them as she could. Luckily it was cold outside and in the church, so she pulled the scarf that was at her throat to cover her mouth.

When the time for communion came and rows and rows of parishioners began filing to the altar, Maria rose with them. She stood at the altar rail and when Father Avila stood before her to give communion, Maria lowered her scarf and looked the priest in the eye. She could see him flinch when he recognized her and he looked around the large space of the church, but there was no one watching him and anyway, there was no way he could signal that Maria was here. People filed back to their seats, but some of the smaller children were antsy and one baby started crying. Maria took the chance to follow them down the side aisle right out of the church. It took only a few minutes to get back to the corner of her street, but she saw one of the small cars with the dark windows stopped a few houses from hers. The car was running, but no one came out or got in it. She waited just another minute or two and kept going up the street. She went into one of the yards that was behind her house and opened the gate that they had made when they put the fence in many years ago. Before she went to her back door, she took a look in the greenhouse just in case someone was hiding there. No one. She went quietly into her house by the back door. The house was quiet, but she was still cautious.

Slowly Maria went to the door to the cellar and opened it. There was Connie and Gloria having coffee and watching the Mass in Portuguese on the large TV. She knocked on the wall so they would hear her coming. "I will be back *un minuto.*" She looked in every space in her sewing room, the dining room and living room. She checked that the front door had not been opened then went upstairs, even looking under beds and in the closets. When she was satisfied that no one had entered, she joined the ladies downstairs. Years ago Gus had put an alarm under the kitchen door mat. It was just a bell that rang downstairs and in the sewing room when someone stepped on the rug inside the back door. Maria had never turned it on, but she did now.

She told Connie if she wanted to leave now, that was fine because she was home for the evening now, but of course she could stay since it was evening now. Connie did want to go home, though. She had canaries in the basement near the wine room. They made a mess throwing around the seed and she had to sweep the floor twice a day. "That is good, *vai p'ra casa*, Connie, *gracias.* Go home." "Wait," Maria stopped Connie on her way out the door. "It is cold now, here, *pega,*" Maria handed Connie a shawl to keep her warm on her walk for the few blocks to her home. She watched Connie walk out of her back door and she could see her leaving the yard from the dining room windows. Gloria asked if she could watch TV downstairs while Maria cooked supper. "Yes, ok," Maria had something she wanted to do while she was alone anyway. First she called Gus' phone again. No answer again. She took a chance and called Gus' house in Montreal. One of his sons answered but Maria could not recognize the voice and the house was noisy. She asked for Gus.... "Gus home? This is Tia Maria."

"Nobody here but me and Nathan and some friends. We are playing video games." "Where your father is?" Maria was hoping he had been up in Canada. "I dunno. He was here yesterday, I think. Maybe 2 days ago. I'll tell Mom you called." "No, do not bother her." "I think she is staying out tonight, but ok then. Bye." Maria sighed.

Maria took some small bottles that she had in a coffee can in the pantry behind several other cans. She went into the basement to retrieve a small bottle of wine which she now kept locked up. When she had opened the wine, she poured herself a glass. She used her kitchen scissors and cut open the tiny plastic bottles and dumped them into the wine bottle and replaced the cork. She placed the bottle in the china cabinet in the dining room and stuck a bow on it. Maria made a quick supper, she and Gloria ate and had a quiet evening.

Early the next morning, Maria called Julia. She asked her if she was going to Mass. Of course, she said and she was leaving in a few minutes. "*O que e'?* What happens?" Julia asked. "I need to go to Mass. You stay with Gloria?" "Did you not go to church yesterday?" "Yes. Can you come?" Maria asked. "Yes, in an hour," Julia did not question. In an hour or so Julia walked into Maria's house. She had stopped at the bakery and placed the warm bread that she brought on the kitchen counter. Maria was ready to leave for church. "Coffee ready. Gloria still sleeps downstairs," Maria said as she rushed out the door as she tied on her black kerchief and although it was not as cold as last evening, she also draped her scarf around her neck.

Walking again along Rivet Street to church, Maria met up with several others on their way to the 10 a.m. service. Into the main front doors again Maria walked straight up the center aisle. Today she sat in the front row. Just in case she was not noticed, when time came for communion, she was the first to pop out of her seat and stood at the altar rail. Father Avila actually did not recognize her until he stood before her, host in hand, he froze for a few seconds holding the white wafer right in front of Maria's face. She smiled, accepted the host, turned and left straight down the center aisle she had entered by and out the doors. The small round figure that she was stood out even more on the deserted street in the cold, bright sunlight. Maria walked straight to her front door and up the steps. She did see the small black car with tinted windows that was parked several houses away, but she knew they saw her as it made a U-turn and came back by her house slowly.

It took only a moment to get to the front door. As soon as she tried to open the front door, the alarm reminded Maria that Gus had set an alarm to her front door too. When she had disarmed it, she hurried into the kitchen where Julia and Gloria were ready to confront the intruder whom they thought had triggered the alarm. "*Todo bem*, it ok," Maria went back one last time to check out the front window. No small dark cars, but Gina's car was pulling up. Maria watched as Gina got out of her car and from the passenger's door came Gus. He was too thin, Maria thought as he walked right up the front steps behind her, several steps behind her. Maria ran over to Gus with a hug that nearly knocked him down, "I cannot reach you for a long time." "You ok?" Gus answered, "You did not hear from me for months sometimes. Why are you worried now? I have been running back and forth to Canada getting things finished for the divorce." "You do not call." Gina sighed as Gus gave Maria a hug and lifted her like a child.

"You stay here tonight?" Maria held his arm as tightly as she could. Even though he was thinner, his biceps were still very thick, but he got the message. "I will be here later," he said. "I came for a change of clothes, I need some work clothes," he said as he ran up the stairs. Maria did not wait for Gina to speak. "We wait in the kitchen. Julia and Gloria having coffee. You have some too." The coffee was hot and strong, but other than the clinking of spoons, the room was totally quiet. Maria asked Gina if she was still helping Nelson with this mother's care. "How Matilda is doing?" she asked. Gina patted her lips with a napkin before speaking, "She is doing well. Some days she talks quite a lot, mostly about the old days. Her husband, oh and your husband too," she looked Maria in the eye and Maria immediately knew what she meant. It seemed that Gina did not know Maria well enough to know that she did not do well with threats or blackmail. "Julia, you can go home now," Maria stood up and took Gina's cup to the sink. "Tomorrow is when you take care of Inez's baby for me. Do you remember?" "Yes, yes," Julia answered, but caring for babies was not work for Julia. She did not mind that Maria did not want babies in her house while Gloria was still there. "I will go make food for Antonio and me. *Adeus.*" She gave Maria a kiss on each cheek and gathered her sweater and purse. "Go out from the back door, please," Maria asked. Usually everyone did so Julia thought nothing of it. Connie left also and Maria stepped out onto the front porch to get a better view of the street as the two ladies left. No small dark cars and no one walking the sidewalk to follow either of them.

XVI

Back in the kitchen, Maria handed Gloria a bowl of some fruit, some St. Jorge cheese and a bag with some fresh bread and she asked her if she would mind waiting downstairs, she would be there shortly. "I see you downstairs and we will eat and watch television." Gloria went downstairs, then Maria opened the back door, held it open, and unwelcomed Gina to leave, "Gina, please tell my brother to call me. I need to talk to Gloria about some plans..*Adeus.*" It took only a moment for Gina to decide it was in her better interest to just leave without addressing the invitation to leave.

Before she joined Gloria downstairs, she tried to call Gus. No answer. She called Connie and asked if she would be available to keep company with Matilda when Nelson had to work. She told her that Gina was preparing to take another one of her shopping trips to New York or somewhere and would not be in town to help with Matilda.

Of course, she said. Her days were free and Matilda was no problem. Just before she said goodnight, she did mention that she was going to say a rosary because she thought she saw a ghost on her way home. She had seen a shadow disappear into her backyard as she approached her house. She called out for Manny but there was no answer. "You come to my house tonight," Maria said. "Come out when I get in front of your house." Without thinking, Maria grabbed her car keys and went to her car before she remembered that Gloria was in the basement waiting for her. She went back and locked the doors to the house and left. There was no one to be seen near her house, along the street to Connie's house or near Connie's house. It took only a moment for Connie to come out and get into the car. She had a large purse with her and once in the car, she reached into the outside pocket and pulled out the gun Maria had given her earlier. "*O que*? What you do with that?" "You give to me when I stayed with Gloria, remember?" Maria took it carefully before they drove off. She checked the safety and put it into her pocket.

It had only been less than 5 minutes since she had left home, but she saw Gina's car at the curb in front of her house when they got there. "Connie, come with me. We go in the front door." Keys in hand, Maria went up the front stairs, but the door was unlocked. Connie never noticed Maria's mind switch gears, but in a split second, Maria was prepared to do what it would take to defend herself, Connie and even Gloria. She slipped her hand into her pocket and undid the safety on the gun. Connie was not sure if she should be frightened, but she followed closely behind Maria. No one in the living room, no one in the dining room and into the kitchen... there was Gus! "Where is Gina?" Maria barked. "Hey, hold on!" Gus smiled. "Why were the doors locked? I have Gina's car. Good thing I still have a key. Where were you? I told you I would stay here tonight." Maria did not answer, but went straight to the door to the basement. "Gloria, you ok?" "I was falling asleep on the couch waiting for you," she answered. Gus went closer to the basement door, "I did not know someone was here. You left that woman here alone? You will be lucky if you still have your silverware and anything else. You know she is a thief, right? And a drug addict?" "How you know anything?" Maria was getting angry. Gus just noticed that Connie was with Maria. "Oh, hello, Connie. You ok? I sure miss the old days with Manny before.. uh, when he was younger." "He was good one time. He is no more," Connie answered and she walked over to the basement door and escaped downstairs.

Gus turned to Maria and shrugged, "Sorry." Maria shoved Gus, "I no know you anymore. How you talk like this to Connie? You go upstairs now to bed. I have too much things to do. No more *bebida* (drink) for you. Go." Maria waited until she heard Gus walking upstairs before she went down to the basement to Gloria and Connie. "Connie, it is good you are here," she whispered. Gloria had not even opened the couch to a bed before she fell asleep. "Gus upstairs. He's no good with Gloria. He don't like her. Plenty of food here or upstairs in the big kitchen. You eat. Tomorrow better things happen."

Maria slept lightly. Her room was closer to the stairs and she wanted to know if Gus tried to give Gloria any grief. Maria woke early and from the kitchen window she saw Susanna quietly getting the grain and feeding chickens and fresh water to the rabbits. After she fed them, Maria tapped on the kitchen window and asked her to come into the kitchen. Susanna brought a bag in with her. She told Maria she was just going to put it into the box on the front porch. There were several black dresses and blouses. She reminded Maria that it was already 6 months since her brother Antonio had died so she did not need to wear black any longer, but she was sure Connie or Julia might need them.. or Maria if she wanted to alter anything she could have them also. Maria poured her some coffee and placed a plate with some cookies called *Marias* that would be great with the coffee. Susanna thanked her, but she could not stay much longer. She had a shift at Dunkin' in an hour. "I will feed and clean animals tomorrow you do not need to come for them. I call you if I need help. *Obrigado,* thank you," Maria took a rabbit from the freezer and one of the bottles of wine from the cabinet near the sewing room and gave them to Susanna. After only one cup of coffee, Susanna got up to leave. Maria walked her to the back door, gave a kiss on each cheek and a hug and thanked her again for helping with the animals for the past few weeks. Maria went to the front door as quickly as she could. She called out to Susanna who was already a few houses away. When she got back to the front steps of Maria's house, Maria told her to go to see Steph at Scissor Wizards on Dartmouth Street. Maria would pay for whatever she needed... haircut, bleach, blow out, manicure, pedicure ...Anything. Susanna was much more pleased than she was about a frozen dead rabbit. The wine was always good, though, and she was thankful for that too.

Maria heard some footsteps and talking upstairs. Gus must be talking on his phone and walking around. Gus came slowly down the stairs and was still on the phone but he ended the call when he got to the doorway to the kitchen. "Gina needs to run some errands. I am going to drive her so I can use her car later." "*Vai la*, you go. I can do things," Maria said, poured herself another cup of coffee and sat at the table waiting for him to leave, but he turned on his way out. "It's not that I don't want to help with whatever you need, so I will be back to help." He came back into the room and planted a kiss on Maria's forehead and left.

As soon as the door closed behind Gus, Maria went to sit with Gloria and Connie. She brought the whole pot of coffee and a platter of *malasadas* and they drank the strong coffee and ate the sugary dough and talked. Maria told Gloria that she was glad for her that she felt better, but the next decision was hers. She could continue with the lifestyle that had gotten her here or find a safe place to give herself a new beginning. If she wanted to go to a rehab, they would call around and get her to one or she could go on her own, but keep in mind, she warned her that Todd and his friends would not forget and forgive what she owed. Maria held tightly onto Gloria's hand. People like that will kill you even if it was just to set an example, she told her. The plans to get her to Canada or send her away by boat would probably not work now, but she could drive her to Maine or New York or wherever she wanted to go. Connie spoke up and added that she could go along if they wanted company.

Gloria was nodding and agreeing with Maria as she spoke. She looked very serious. Could she make some phone calls and she would have some answers soon. Maria took Connie's arm. "Give 'by herself time' to her. We go upstairs. I will call Nelson. If he works today, you stay with Matilda." Connie nodded. Gloria was on the house phone, Maria assumed, so she got her cell phone to call Nelson but he did not have to work until tomorrow, he said.

In a short while, Gloria came slowly up the stairs. She had a paper in her hand that she gave Maria. "I can stay at this address. One stop before I leave town." "Yes, very good," Maria answered. She had already started to gather the food and drink for what might be a few hours of driving around to who knows where. She went to the kitchen cupboard where she kept some wine. She cringed when she put some plastic cups along with the wine into a canvas tote. Maria went into her back yard for a moment, took a few deep breaths and a look around the yard and went back in to gather everyone. The three of them were getting settled in Maria's car when her cell phone rang in her bag. She managed to fish it out and answer it without losing the call. It was Nelson. Was there any chance that Connie or Maria could stay with Matilda? He had gotten an emergency call to report to help with a large fire up on Acushet Avenue in the north end. Did Maria want him to try to call Gina, she had been very helpful lately? No, Maria told him that Gina was not going to be available, but she could bring Connie by the house now.

Since Matilda's house was close by, it only took a few minutes to drop Connie off. Maria reached into her pocket to read the address that Gloria had given her and realized the paper was on the kitchen counter.

She drove to the side of her house. It was chancy to be back and forth in the neighborhood with Gloria in the car, but she was only going to take a moment. She left Gloria in the car. Gus was sitting at the table. "How you are here? I leave here only minutes," Maria grabbed the paper off the counter. "Gina has other things to do, so I can go with you if you want. I told Gina I could do some yard work for you." Gus put his hand on Maria's shoulder. She told him she was driving Gloria away and he offered to go along since Connie was busy. "Really let me help you, I owe you. I don't give a shit about Gloria, but I do want to help you." Maria gave Gus a kiss on the cheek, "Come now. Ok?" Gus sat in the driver's seat to drive and Maria put the canvas tote in the back seat with Gloria who had a hoodie on pulled up over her head and dark glasses. Maria's cell phone rang again. Maria answered with a sigh, "*O que e*? What is?" It was Connie and it seemed that it was not a good day for Matilda.

Gus put his hand on Maria's wrist. "You go help. Let me do this for you." Maria put her other hand on Gus's and just nodded. She felt in her pocket to give him the paper that Gloria had given her with the address where she would be staying. She also felt the gun that she had left in her pocket last night. She still might need it today. Gus drove Maria to Matilda's house. She gave him a kiss on each cheek, patted his hand that was on the steering wheel and got out holding open the door for Gloria to get into the front seat and they drove away. Connie came to the front door before Maria even got to the front steps and Matilda almost flew past them out the door. Matilda was screeching so loud that Maria could not understand what Connie was trying to say to her. Matilda screamed, "They are coming. They know what we have done. Maria help me." Connie could not speak any more. She was crying and shaking. Matilda was wielding an umbrella like she would a sword, but Maria walked over to her. She pulled the umbrella from Matilda's hand, gave a tight hug and as she relaxed, Maria gave a kiss on each cheek. In a few seconds, Matilda was the quiet, skinny mouse that everyone knew.

"I will get tea," Maria said as she sat Matilda onto the sofa, she pat her on the head. Connie was still shaken and sat quietly.

The kettle whistled and Maria poured the hot water into the cups. Crack! One of the cups cracked and the hot water spilled everywhere. Maria wiped the hot water then brought the tea to Matilda and Connie. In a short while Maria sent Connie home. It might be only an hour or two before Nelson returned. Maria sat with Matilda. She held her hand and soon Matilda began to speak in Portuguese to Maria. She asked if Maria thought anyone would find out their secret. "Jose' e Nuno?" Matilda whispered. Maria patted her hand and stroked her hair a few times to soothe and comfort her. She asked if Maria knew if their secrets had been discovered. "*Descansa,os dois mortos* (relax both dead)," Maria whispered back to her, and Matilda nodded, "*Sim, sim, mortos os dois* (yes, yes, both dead)," she answered, "*Deus perdoa, Deus abencoi* (God forgive, God bless)." Maria kissed Matilda's forehead and patted her hand. With a tear in his eye, Matilda looked up to Maria, "*Tenho saudades dos dias passados* (I long for the days of the past)." Maria responded, "*Tenho saudades de o que podia ser* (I long for what could have been)."

Matilda insisted on asking if anyone was watching them or if they were in danger. Maria made another cup of *maracuja* (passion flower tea) and by the time Nelson arrived Matilda was quiet and relaxed. Nelson came into the house in uniform and Matilda hugged him several times, thanking him for saving them. A tear did come to Nelson's eye when he realized his mother did not know who he was, but he squatted down to look her in the eye and said, "*Nao e' nada.*" (It's nothing,) He kissed her forehead and took her hand and walked her out the back door. He asked her to sit on the old wicker chair and said he would be right back. When he returned to Maria, he thanked her in Portuguese and English, "I should start paying you ladies for staying with my mother. I want to keep her out of the hospitals, but there is not a day now that she can be alone, not even an hour. The yard is fenced and the gate is locked, but she can be very alert sometimes. All she can get into is the greenhouse or back into the kitchen." He took out his wallet, but Maria pushed his hand away so quickly that he realized he had insulted her. "*Para a alma do meu Jose' e do teu pai Nuno,*" (For the souls of my Jose and your father Nuno,) He nodded. Maria left walking and on her way back to her house she thought -—she thought a lot. That was probably the first time in years that she had even mentioned her husband's name, never mind that she did an act of charity for his soul. She hoped that it was making a difference. Now it was time to put the thought of him away again.

XVII

Maria walked quickly to her house. She walked around the house and made certain that everything was as it should be. The first thing she did in her kitchen was call Gus. She knew he always had his phone ready. The cord from her phone reached across her kitchen and she went to the pantry and took a gallon jug off the bottom shelf. That was the special wine. No answer. She hung up the phone and went back to the kitchen counter. She took a cinnamon stick from its jar into a large coffee mug and poured the wine. She stirred the wine with the cinnamon as she walked to the front porch. Outside she lit her cheroot and tried to put her feet up on the porch rail. She was too short, so she just rocked the chair, maybe this would help her think. The house phone rang and she ran in to get it. It was Gloria. In a raspy voice, "Come help us. We are Riverside Park." Maria tried to ask if Gus was there, if there had been an accident, no answer, but she could hear a lot of noise. She checked her pocket and released the safety on the gun, poured her wine into an empty glass soda bottle that Gloria had left behind and went quickly to get her car. She forgot Gus had her car. Julia must still have Jacinto's car in her yard. She also knew that Julia would not drive the car, but keep it as a shrine with tires.

Very soon she was at Julia's door, but she heard the voices of children in the backyard. There was Julia playing with the children. Maria sat with her and asked her for the favor of using Jacinto's car. "*Por favor* (Please.)" Julia ran into the house and got the keys. "*Certo, Madrinha*," Julia handed the keys to Maria with a kiss on each cheek. Two of the children were squealing and Julia had to run over to them. Maria blew another kiss and got into Jacinto's car. It did not smell musty as she thought it might. It smelled of lavender and Spic and Span. Julia must come out and wash the car inside and out. As she pulled away from Julia's yard, she remembered to check if she had been followed. She saw a small black car with tinted widows pull away from the curb. It followed for a few blocks, but turned up County Street.

They had business, but she was not today's business this time. Maria knew where she had to go, but she took Front Street in case Gus had gone by the docks with Gloria.

She drove along the cove and took the side street through the old mills to Front Street. There were other boys on bikes, small cars, but their dealings were with the patients at the methadone clinic. There were a few police cars parked in empty lots along her route, but it seemed they were sleeping or just watching for speeders. Down along the waterfront most of the fishing boats were in. Good, if Gus needed help, she could come back here and find some of her friends or friends of Joe and Nuno. There she was thinking of them again. Their friends would not be hanging out here.

She got to Riverside Park. Maria saw a car that she recognized pulling away from the far side of the park. There was one car left and that was hers. Usually the whole park was busy, but there were no kids on bikes, skateboards or skates, no smaller kids on swings... no one. Oh, one little, old man sitting on a bench feeding the pigeons. He had bread or seeds in a paper sack and reached in every few seconds and sprinkled crumbs and seeds in small piles on the ground. She parked her car right on the grass and walked quickly across the skate park. She stood several feet away from her car waiting. Waiting to see if anyone came, followed, moved, but nothing but the little old man sitting a few feet from her feeding non-existent pigeons. "You should check on the people in that car. No one has moved since the Lincoln drove away. I don't think they are making love in there," he said in his gravelly voice and walked away to sit at a bench further away.

Maria walked cautiously to her car. She came up on the passenger door and looked in the open window. "*Força Mulher*" she thought to herself as she reached in to touch Gloria's bloody throat to feel for some heartbeat, but nothing. She closed her eyes for a moment to regain whatever strength she could muster and walked around the car to check on Gus. He needed a haircut was her first thought seeing his head against the steering wheel. She brushed the wisp of hair from his brow and he moaned, very softly, "Maria, get us out of here." He coughed and spit a mouthful of blood that spattered on the windshield. She leaned in as far as she could, kissed her fingertips and touched the kiss to his forehead. She went quickly back to Jacinto's car, drove it off the grass and up the small lane to park it beside her own car. She opened the passenger door of the car to try to pull Gloria into Jacinto's car. The pigeon man was suddenly there and lifted Gloria, put her behind the wheel, closed the car door and was gone before Maria could ask what he was doing or why. Taking no time to think, she squeezed into her own car beside her bloody brother. There was blood everywhere. She pulled the sleeves of her big, black, man's sweater over her hands to hold the steering wheel. Back at her house she drove her car right around to the back of the house over grass and garden.

She opened the back door of the house and did her best to drag Gus out and onto the kitchen floor. She poured a pitcher of water over him and used towels to wipe away blood. He had a gash across his forehead but it was not too deep. "*Cabeca de nabo*," (turnip head), she muttered as she ripped open his shirt. One bullet in his shoulder. She packed a few cold wet towels on his shoulder and ripped more clothing off him to find any other wounds. She turned him to check his back. "*Ai, mulher.... Aiiii*" (Ow, woman! Owww) At least she got a response from him. No holes in his back, but the bullet might be in the bone at his shoulder. Maria hurried to the phone. She called Julia, but asked Julia if she could speak to her husband Antonio. Of course, Julia called Antonio to the phone and Maria told him what she needed to say and what they needed to do for her. Then she called Suzanna and prepared her kitchen for surgery.

With precision and efficiency Julia arrived then Suzanna with her daughter. No questions about what to do. Suzanna's daughter worked in the ER and knew what to do.... Maria had gotten the motor starting spray cans from the greenhouse. She handed them to Rose, Suzanna's daughter. Rose turned the first can over to read ingredients and she said, "Where did you get this? This Champion stuff is 80% ether, we have to be careful, but we could use this to help with surgery. I will need more towels and as much gauze as you can find, some alcohol too and do you have a filet knife from when you clean small fish. Do you have the white aprons that you use when you are canning and maybe some white t-shirts? Also I will need some white quilting thread and a couple of sewing needles. Do you have what they call needle-nose pliers?" Maria already knew the starter spray was high in ether, but not a time to talk right now. She left the room and quickly returned with at least half a dozen white t-shirts that were whiter than the day she had bought them. The aprons were always bleached and wrapped in tissue ready to start canning. The sewing supplies were in her workroom and the pliers in the kitchen drawer with a few other tools. While she was getting these things together and wiping everything with a lot of alcohol, Rose had dragged the kitchen table to the middle of the room, put the leaf in the table and sprayed bleach or alcohol on walls and she and Julia had wiped counters and walls quickly. Together they all put Gus on the table and washed him well.

Everyone went into bathrooms and washed, put on the white aprons and t-shirts. A moment before they began the surgery, the phone rang. "Use a towel to pick up the phone," Rose told Maria. It was Antonio, "It is done. Jacinto's car is home," he said then hung up.

It did not take long to remove the bullet. The shattered bone would take more than her skill to repair, but he would be ok. She stitched Gus's face where a bullet had torn across his forehead. Carefully everyone carried Gus downstairs and as quickly as they had all come, they left one at a time, front and back doors. With Gus settled, Maria went out to her car and washed and sterilized it inside and out. She brought the paper sack that she found under the seat into the house and into the wine cellar. After the bleach she used the hose on the front floor and seats, then the wet/dry vac. She left the car doors open to air out the car then she sprayed the car inside with a mist of hydrogen peroxide. Gus and Gloria were safe, but more work to be done soon.

With her kitchen smelling more of bleach than it ever had, Maria put her gallon of bleach on the counter and poured herself a large glass of wine. She took another look in on Gus. He was fine. Rose would be back in a while to check on him again. Maria went to her front door, checked that no one was around, no cars, no bikes and she checked in the box where tailoring and sewing requests were left for her. She brought the two envelopes that she found there to the backyard. She did not need to be seen. She brought her glass of wine and cheroot to the wicker rocking chair that was under the arbor. There were a few grapes that had escaped being eaten or picked. She put a few beside her ashtray and lit the cheroot while she checked the notes from the sewing box. There was a thank you note for Matilda and her for the dresses they had altered for the most recent wedding. There also was an envelope with Gus's name written in a handwriting she recognized immediately. She took a large swallow of her wine. The handwritten note read, "*Lamento muito a sua perda (*I am very sorry for your loss)." Maria smirked. There were very few people who knew anything that happened today. She knew that everyone she had called for help could be trusted. That only left whose hand was on the grip of the gun then drove away in that Lincoln or who had sent them.

Maria finished her cheroot and her glass of wine and went back into the house. She had thrown a bag of Gus's clothes into the sewing room. She had planned to burn everything in the morning. She spread some tissue paper on the floor and dumped the contents of the bag. She found what she was looking for, Gus's phone. There was a knock on the front door. Maria went cautiously to answer the door. It was Rose. "Come, come in fast." Maria did not want anyone to see the comings or goings at her house, but she had forgotten to tell Rose to cut through the backyard to her back door. They checked on Gus and

Maria decided to sleep in the basement to watch and help him, but he recovered from the ether well and was in pain, but recovering.

Julia came over early the next morning. She came to stay with Gus since Maria told her she had important things to do. Julia did not ask. Gus was alert and getting restless. Maria went downstairs to see Gus before she left. "You shower, you eat, no phone, no leave the cellar. You stay." Gus knew better than to question Maria's orders. When she left, Maria went by Nelson Castro's house. No car, she cut through yards and walked leaving her car home. It was early, but she knew it was the best time of day for Matilda. Matilda was sitting with a *tjela* (extra large cup) of coffee and slice of *massa* (Portuguese sweet bread). "*Queres café'? Come,* (Want coffee? Eat)," Just as Maria sat, Nelson came into the kitchen. He bent over and gave his mother a kiss on her forehead. "*Meu filho vai para escola agora.* (My son is going to school now)," Matilda patted her son on his arm.

"Sit down with my mother for coffee, I made a pot a few minutes ago. You are here earlier than Gina usually comes. Connie said Gina is going shopping in New York or Boston again. Do you want to stay for a while? I was going to let her ride with me up to Lowe's. She has been talking about fixing the floor in the greenhouse. I am just going to get a couple of bags of mulch or something for the floor in there. It would give her some peace of mind. Gina said she goes out there to sit for at least an hour a day." Maria nodded, "*Vai, vai la,* (Go ahead, go)." Nelson left the two women at the kitchen table having their coffee, coffee strong enough to bring the dead back to life.

As soon as he left, Maria had Matilda put on a sweater and brought her outside to the greenhouse. The door was still not fixed. Just one gentle tug and the screws pulled out of the rotted wood, the hasp to the ground and the door creaked open. There was a milk crate under the crumbled potting bench that Maria pulled out for Matilda to sit on and she took her hand. She sat quietly for a few moments and then Matilda looked around. Like a switch had been flipped, Matilda was the Matilda of 30 years ago. She started talking to Maria in Portuguese. "I know Nuno was here yesterday. I know it was him and your Joe out here. They were supposed to be out for 10 days. Why are they here?" She no longer looked like the frail little widow. She picked up the small garden shovel and started to dig up the floor. "There is blood here. No one must know," Matilda was getting frantic... and just like that, her energy left her and she sat down again on the milk crate looking like a sad little girl. Maria had cared for friends and even her own mother when she had dementia, so this was not a surprise. "We can go in the house now," Maria took Matilda's arm and helped her up. They stepped out of the greenhouse and Maria pushed the screws back into their holes on the door frame. When they turned to go back into the house, the phone in Maria's pocket rang. Strange ring. It was Gus's phone. Maria put her handkerchief over the phone and answered.

"*Diga* (speak)," Maria answered in the deepest Gus-like voice she could. "Gus, I will go by your sister's house to see you in half an hour." Even if she could have figured out how to read the caller ID, she would not have needed it to know who this was calling Gus. She had hoped that leaving the house early she could slow the spread of gossip and it looked like it was working. Nelson returned with the mulch he had bought. Maybe it was a good thing that he had bought the redwood mulch. That should look just right on the greenhouse floor.

Maria left and went to her house. She cut through yards and went to her back door which she had locked for a change. When she came into the kitchen, Julia was there making some breakfast. She told Maria that Gus was very pale, but he seemed to be doing well. "*Bom* (good), you stay down stairs with Gus. Gina coming here. I need to talk to her." Julia took the platter of food. "Gus feels warm, I close the heat, but I am cold." "Here is my sweater," Maria took off the black cardigan that she wore and put it over Julia's shoulders. The black sweater was heavy, long and had big pockets. Anyone would be warm in that sweater even in the snow.

Maria unlocked the front door and sat at the dining table. Gina walked in but stopped short. It took a moment for her to think of what to say. "Y-you?" was all she managed. She brushed her sleeve as though she were getting rid of a bug. "Where is Gus? What are you doing here? I heard you had had an accident. I thought he might need help if you were hurt." "You hear that where? Was it Father Avila? Or his boyfriend Todd? Sit down, Gina. Talk to me," Maria said as she slid an empty cup and the coffee pot across the table. Gina sat but did not touch the coffee or the cup. "Where is Gus? Is he hurt? I saw your car outside. Where is Gloria?" Maria drank her coffee, black, strong and hot then she refilled her cup. No one spoke. Gina shouted, "Where is Gloria? Where is Gus?" The door to the basement opened, Gina looked up and saw Julia. "Where did you come from?" Gina said louder than she needed to for anyone to hear even if they were a block away.

"I came to help with sewing," Julia said softly and calmly. Julia went into the sewing room and sat at the sewing machine. Gina answered coolly, "I heard there was an accident last evening with a car that looked like hers and I came to see how Maria is. I was very worried." Maria was still sipping her coffee, "Very nice you are worried," she said between sips. Gina answered, "I know you are not happy with me. You probably think I will hurt your brother, but I will not. I am worried that I have not heard from Gus yet and I was truly concerned when I heard that you were hurt." Gina got up quickly, gave Maria a kiss on each cheek and left. "Judas," Maria whispered. She waited for Gina to leave before she got up from the table. She went to the front porch to watch Gina drive away. She saw her drive away and then a glimpse of a big, black Lincoln drive away from the other corner.

Maria sighed. She went to check on Gus. When she got downstairs, he was pacing. "What the hell happened yesterday? Oh, shit! Is that Gloria dead? That pimp or whatever he is came over to her car window and started shooting. She could not have made it. What happened to me? It felt like a flamethrower blew up my shoulder... oh, and my head!" Maria sat him on the couch, "You rest. Rosa coming to check you." Gus leaned back and reclined his seat, "Now what?" Maria patted him on his knee, she did not want to pat his head with all those bandages around his forehead. "I will fix it," Maria assured. Julia came in with Rosa. They would care for Gus, so Maria went upstairs, but when she returned, she thanked Rosa and Julia, kissed each of her friends on both cheeks and sent them home. She had a few questions for Gus. He had new bandages and was eating so he was fine. Maria asked Gus where was the paper that Gloria had written the address for Gus and how did they get to the park on Riverside? Gus covered his face with his right hand, shed a few tears then looked up at Maria. "You cry from pain?" Maria gently brushed his hair off the bandage across his brow. Gus gave a little laugh, "You are tough, *hermana* (sister)." Maria insisted, "*Diga* (tell me), what address on the paper and why Riverside Park?" "What happened to Gloria? She could not have lived," Gus answered. "We have no time for this. Why the park?" Maria grabbed Gus's arm and shook it.

"Gloria asked to stop there before we drove away. We were going to go to Falmouth, but she said she had to say goodbye to someone. We waited there on the maintenance path near the trees. A big, black, old Lincoln pulled up on the passenger side. She opened her window and all I saw was a silencer on the barrel of a gun fire. It must have hit her 3 or 4 times in the face and neck. I could not see who was shooting, it was so fast and the person was tall. They kept firing even when she fell forward and that is how I got hit. They were gone before I knew it. It was not like you would see in a movie. The blood was spraying everywhere. I think I could smell it." Maria patted his knee. "You are ok, but you do not call anybody. I do a few things and then I come back. You stay down here. Do you want Antonio or Duarte to come stay with you?" "Duarte? I have not seen him in years. I thought he moved to California." "Yes, but he visits *familia* this week. I call Duarte. He will come." One phone call to Julia's house and in less than half hour, Duarte Medeiros was at the door. He was Julia's brother. Maria showed him to the basement.. She knew he would be able to settle any situation that came up. He looked like a Portuguese grizzly bear, a big friendly bear until he got crossed. There was enough food and drink and a large screen tv with soccer playoffs playing for the men to have no need to leave the house for days, but Maria knew it would only be hours.

Gus was good, but Maria gave Duarte instructions anyway. She showed him where she kept extra food besides what was in the pantry cupboards and refrigerator and where the extra wine and beer was kept. She reminded them not to go upstairs for any reason. Before leaving, Maria decided to move her car. She parked right in front of the house and locked all the outside doors on the house. There was a light rain and Maria just tied her kerchief tighter and left the house walking toward the church. She walked to the front steps of Mt. Carmel Church, she blessed herself and walked up the side street, Bonney Street, to the front door of the rectory. The big, black Lincoln that she recognized as Father Avila's car was parked right out front. No going in through the kitchen this time, right up the front steps and in through the front door.

Maria turned the door handle but the rectory door was locked. It was never locked during the day. She rang the bell several times. Not a housekeeper or even a secretary answered the door. She heard loud voices and she heard some scuffling around. It took a moment, but when the door did open it was Todd and he stood half behind the door. He was shirtless and shoeless and not looking arrogant at all. He actually looked like he was looking at a ghost. "He is in his office," Todd said almost in a whisper. Maria flung open the office door expecting to see the great, Father Sergio Avila standing indignantly to face her. Instead she found a weepy, scared, sad excuse for a priest sitting on a footstool with his head in his hands. Maria shook him, "Get up. *Faz de conta* (make believe) you a man." Sergio sobbed, "I thought you were dead, they said you were killed yesterday. I don't want you dead. You are my oldest friend." Maria clucked, "Tsk, crazy, you crazy. We no friends and I am *muito viva* (very alive). Who say I die?"

Sergio sighed and was about to speak when Todd pushed open the door and entered the room. He was dressed now and did not look scared in the least. He stood just inside the door glaring at Sergio, "You have a meeting soon, we need to leave." Sergio dried his eyes on his shirttail and stood, "Of course," he said. He was now Father Avila again. He patted Maria on her shoulder, "I am glad you are fine." Maria walked to the front door, but she could hear Sergio and Todd still talking in the office. All she could make out was, "Yeah, she should have been dead. She was in the car with Gloria."

The light rain was not so light any more. It was raining heavily. She did not have much more time before gossip and curiosity started dangerous rumors. Gina was already looking for word from Gus and others would be asking for him too. Kids from the skate park would talk.

XVIII

Gina went back in through her front door, straight through her front room, dining room and to the door to the basement. She knocked loudly, there was no answer... she tried again and soon she heard the bolts unlocking the door. As Duarte opened the door, Maria could hear the two of them shouting, The soccer match was blasting on the tv. Benfica was playing Manchester and it looked like Duarte and Gus had a party going on. They were both wearing Benfica tanks over their shirts. Well, she did not have to worry about Gus's recovery. Maria asked Duarte when he had to go back to Julia's house, but he said there was no problem with him staying the whole day. He did have to go to Mass with her and Antonio in the morning. Tomorrow was an anniversary Mass for the loss of Jacinto. He said that Julia could probably bring his church clothes and he could stay all night. It was not long before Rosa came by again. She showed Maria how to change Gus's bandages on his shoulder and head. She even brought a Benfica bandana to tie over his head bandage. Maria told the two soccer fans they had to stay in the basement and lock the door. That did not bother them at all.

Shortly a quick knock on the kitchen door. Maria realized she had forgotten to unlock the door. She opened it and to Maria's surprise it was Julia and she had Matilda with her. A kiss on each cheek and hugs for Matilda. Maria whispered to Julia when she hugged her and told her Gus was in the basement and Duarte was with him. Julia nodded, "*Esta' bem. (*It's good.) Matilda comes with me now to get the dresses for wedding. Only 3 *semanas* (weeks) for wedding. Last fit for them." "Don't go now ladies." The three women turned at once to see Gina standing in the dining room, "I am still worried about Gus. It has been over a day that I have not heard from him. I have not heard from him and I came to see if he was here. You would not hide him from me, would you Maria? I miss him." "We only talk about more sewing work Matilda will help with. No Augusto here," Julia spoke.

Maria assured Gina she would give Gus the message if she saw him. Maria put the pot of coffee on the dining table and she asked the ladies if they would like some coffee before they left. Julia, Matilda and Maria each picked up a cup. Gina did not pick up a cup or even answer, but blew kisses, turned and left. Before their quick cup of coffee was done, Connie walked in through the front door. She looked around to make sure no one else was around. "Who killed Gloria and hurt Gus will look for Gus and Gloria now. This is bad. Tell us what to do." Maria looked into her coffee cup for a moment as though she were reading her tea leaves, "Sergio's friend did this. We need to make him gone." Although she did not follow the conversation, Matilda was getting anxious. Maria took Matilda's hand, "We will do sewing tomorrow. You go to see Nelson now." Only half the cloud lifted from Matilda's eyes, "Nelson will come soon from school. But Nuno is not there, I think he is dead." The other ladies looked at each other. "Nelson needs his *ceia* (supper). You go home," Maria assured and it was decided that Connie would drive Matilda home. Matilda was totally quiet and calm, "*Tenho frio* (I am cold)," she said softly. Julia still wore Maria's sweater. She took it off and draped it on Matilda's shoulders, gave her a hug and everyone said goodbye to her, kisses and hugs all around.

Maria left for the rectory. She could walk over, but driving through the neighborhood then parking on the street in front of the rectory would make a better statement. She wanted to make sure Todd and maybe even Sergio knew she did not fear them. Maria parked out front, but walked around to the back of the house to enter through the kitchen. She never noticed Gina's car parked on the side of the church. When she walked through the kitchen, she heard voices, voices that she recognized. Gina was talking loudly, "You said she was dead. I believed you. You were probably drunk or high. I have known her for years." Maria was touched by Gina's concern. She always knew Gina to be cold, but at least she cared.

She walked straight through to the office and the holy trio of them , Gina, Sergio and Todd stood with mouths open when Maria appeared in the doorway. Gina came over and gave Maria a hug. "What the hell are you doing here?" Sergio sneered, "Are you here to throw that fight with Gloria in Todd's face again?" Maria laughed, "Sergio you a real fool. Todd has no danger from Gloria." Gina's phone rang in her purse and she stepped out of the room without saying anything. She looked in from the hall, "I have to leave," she said as she quickly rushed out through the kitchen. "Now you tell," Maria said, arms folded across her ample chest, "Why did you try to kill me?" She looked Todd straight in the eye, but Sergio answered, "I would not try to kill you, much as we seldom agree." Maria responded to Sergio, but kept her stare at Todd, "You only try to hurt with words. Todd is not you." Todd returned her stare, "Why would I hurt anyone," he said with a smile of fake-concern. "So, where is Gloria and how is she?" Todd's demeanor was more sinister now. He took a deep breath and stood straighter, taller, like a soldier at attention. Todd spoke impatiently, "Listen, stop playing games with me. Gloria could not have survived the shooting. And you, how did you make it without a scratch? WHERE IS SHE?" Sergio was shaking, possibly with rage. He stood on wobbly legs. Todd turned to him, "Oh sit down you old, pompous queer," and shoved him back into his leather chair. But Todd had made the mistake of turning his back on Maria. She grabbed the precious ornate candle stick from the coffee table and hit Todd so hard across the back of his head that they heard his neck snap as he hit the floor. There was no blood and Sergio could not move, but Maria calmly said, "*Ave' Maria, reza por nos pecadores, agora e na hora da nossa morte. Amen.* (Hail Mary, pray for us sinners now and at the hour of our death. Amen)." Maria went over to Sergio who was still sitting like a lump of putty in his chair. She punched him in his jaw so hard that his lip split open and the red mark from her punch was almost bruised already. "Call *policia,* tell them Todd hurt you and you hit with candle. I know you lie good." She wiped the candlestick and put it in Sergio's hand for a moment, then dropped it on the floor near Todd. She put the phone in his hand and quickly went out to her car and left.

Thank God this was over. Maria drove home. She used her hardly used cell phone and called Julia and Connie to meet her at her house. She did not bother to drive into the yard or beside the house. She parked in front and ran up the stairs and through the house to the kitchen. There in her kitchen was Gina hugging Gus. Maria stopped so fast, she almost fell backwards. "How you here?" "Gus called me," Gina said with a smile, "It is awful that Gloria was so badly hurt again. How is she? Gus is lucky to be alive. I am so glad that everyone who matters is alright." She kissed Gus on his cheek. Duarte was just coming up from the basement, "I guess you don't need me anymore. I will go back to my aunt's house, but call if you need anything." Maria put her arm around his neck, he was so tall that she had to pull his head down to kiss his cheek and whispered a thank you in his ear then gave him a hug although she could only reach half around him. Maria looked at Gus who looked confused. He turned to Gina, "Did I tell you Gloria was hurt?" "Of course, you don't remember?" she kissed his cheek, "You poor thing, I know your head will be better soon." "I want to sit outside. I have not been out of the basement. Can I have a beer, too?" Gus said as he walked out the back door and Gina followed.

The wail of screeching tires then brakes in front of her house, brought Maria running to her front porch. From the back of the house, Gus ran still holding his bottle of beer and Gina carrying her glass of wine. Gus stopped short when he saw the black Lincoln pulled up right to the front steps. Bloody and staggering Todd tumbled out of the car. "You bitch!" spitting blood as he shouted and blood dripping down the back of his head and down his neck. "This is not worth it." Maria thought it was she that Todd was screaming at, but she looked over her shoulder to see that he was looking at Gina in the eye.

Todd pulled a shaky hand from his pocket with a gun in his hand, but he could not steady it easily. Everyone stood still but two shots rang out. Gus went down like a sack of wet cement. Maria ran to him even though Todd's shaky hand still waved the gun as he fell to his knees. Gus moaned as he lay on the ground with blood running from his leg. Gus looked up at Gina, "You know him?" Todd, now on his knees, "Of course she knows me. I work for her." "Shut up! Shut up, you stupid fool!" Gina shouted back.

Todd lay on the ground wasting the last of his strength trying to hold the gun up one more time as Maria tied her kerchief around Gus' leg. Gus looked up at Gina with a new look in his eye. "It was you? I told you where I was going with Gloria. You set us up? You?" Gus winced but pulled himself up leaning on Maria. He pulled back to slap Gina, but Maria grabbed his arm. "No hittin' woman," she said as she slapped Gina herself. Gina took a big swallow of what was left of the wine in her glass and tossed the glass onto the drive, "Another fool!" From the back of the house came Duarte followed by Julia, Connie and trailing behind was Matilda. "I came back like you asked," Duarte said.

"*Tenho frio,* I cold," Matilda said as she pulled the sweater tighter around herself. No one noticed Todd rally enough strength to raise his arm one more time and fire a shot that grazed Gina's head. "*Filho da cadela,* bastard, you will die now. You could have had a good life if you were smart." She tore her expensive silk blouse off and held it to her head as she stepped toward Todd when a shot rang out and she dropped to the ground at Gus' feet.

Matilda stood slowly to her full height and dropped the gun from her thin little hand at Maria's feet, "This was in the pocket of your sweater." Maria slipped the gun into her apron pocket and went to Todd's body, held his hand for a moment and said a short prayer before she walked back to Gus. She pulled him away from Gina's body and waited for the ambulance.

Sirens and blue flashing lights invaded the quiet neighborhood. Maria sat on the drive holding Gus and Connie, Julia and Duarte holding Matilda's hand were sitting on the front porch steps. Nelson jumped out of his car before it was fully stopped and ran to his mother. Matilda hugged her son, "What a nice police officer you are," she said in Portuguese. The ambulance took Gus away. It was so embarrasing, Maria said, that Gina and Todd had a dispute that ended with them killing each other. "*Que desgraca* (what a disgrace)!"

The End

---

[1] slippers

Don't miss out!

Visit the website below and you can sign up to receive emails whenever Madelyn Gregory publishes a new book. There's no charge and no obligation.

https://books2read.com/r/B-A-YKVJB-ALHGD

Connecting independent readers to independent writers.